CROSSING SISTERS

OTHER WORKS BY JESSICA TILLES

NOVELS

In My Sisters' Corner
Apple Tree
Fatal Desire
Loving Simone

SERIES

The Raven Trilogy
Anything Goes
Sweet Revenge
Unfinished Business

ANTHOLOGIES

Erogenous Zone: A Sexual Voyage
(with Bill Holmes, William Fredrick Cooper, et al)

The Triumph of My Soul
(with Elissa Gabrielle, Linda R. Herman, Bill Holmes)

e-QUICKIE

No One Has to Know
(with William Fredrick Cooper — Kindle Edition)

JESSICA TILLES

CROSSING
SISTERS

XPRESS YOURSELF
PUBLISHING, LLC

Xpress Yourself Publishing
P.O. Box 1615
Upper Marlboro, Maryland 20773

ISBN: 978-0-9845273-4-2

Library of Congress Control Number: 2011931271

Cover and Interior Design by TWA Solutions
www.twasolutions.com

Visit our Web site at www.xpressyourselfpublishing.com

BOOKS ARE AVAILABLE AT QUANTITY DISCOUNTS. FOR INFORMATION, PLEASE CONTACT BOOK SALES AT (301) 390-3645 OR WRITE TO BOOK SALES, XPRESS YOURSELF PUBLISHING, P.O. BOX 1615, UPPER MARLBORO, MD 20773.

For the sisters who keep me inspired,
focused and full of laughter

and...

S.L.

ACKNOWLEDGEMENTS

This year of 2011 marks the ten-year anniversary of *Anything Goes*, my debut novel, and my emergence onto the literary scene. It has truly been a PHENOMENAL journey! I have made mistakes and wonderful friendships. If given the opportunity to do it all over again, I would do nothing differently. I humbly give thanks to God for blessing me with passion, dedication, and perseverance to continue my literary career.

Mom and Dad, I miss you terribly and always will.

I feel an Oprah moment coming on. Acquaintances are a dime a dozen, but good friends are hard to find. Each person listed within these acknowledgements I call my friend. You have stuck by me through thick, thin and the in between. You truly had my back when you could have chosen to look in the opposite direction. From the bottom of my heart, I thank you.

Gary Johnson, Publisher of Black Men In America.com, for his friendship, professionalism, and continuously giving me straight advice with no chaser! I have said it several times, and I will say it several times more, his picture should be in the dictionary beside the word friend because he is truly the epitome of friend. He is the best "girlfriend" I have ever had!

Ella Curry of EDC-Creations for being a wonderful friend and colleague. Your honesty and straight-from-the-hip approach keeps me grounded and true to whom I am as an author, publisher, and a person. Your friendship and words of wisdom are priceless, and I take none of it for granted!

ESSENCE® Best-Selling Author Bill Holmes for editing *Crossing Sisters*. It has been five years and you are consistent with your honesty and unwavering friendship through all types of weather. Your kindness and friendship humbles me, and I am so proud to call you my BFF.

William Fredrick Cooper I simply cannot imagine life with you in it! Your love for literature and passion for storytelling continues to inspire me. Your friendship is unwavering.

Harold T. Fisher of WHUR FM 96.3 (yeah, uh huh, yeah!), Eric Pete, John Wooden, Yonder, K. Lowery Moore, Paula Price Tilghman, Wynonna Denise Ware, Mika Barnes, Jo Hawly Chubbs, Nellie Graham, Reggie Ware (thank you for allowing me to use your name, kindness and likeness as a soul mate for Maya) and my Xpress Yourself Publishing family. Thank you all for being an e-mail or phone call away.

Leslie Walker, my sister, best friend, and confidant. Together we have battled some serious storms, which only makes our bond that much stronger. I thank you for always being in your sister's corner, no matter what. Life would be dull without you in it, diva!

Bernice Rowe, my beautiful cousin and surrogate mother, for her unconditional love, unwavering support, friendship, and for being my DIY (do-it-yourself) partner-in-crime. That woman keeps me in Home Depot or Lowe's!

A sincere thank you to all of my family (especially my siblings: Herb Lipscomb, Jacqueline Wright Johnson, Valerie Wright Fleming, Colleen Wright Green and Sheila Wright) for your unconditional love and support.

I would like to send a heart-warming thank you to the book clubs (especially The Jackson Mississippi Readers Club and PeaceinPages), and you, the reader, because you are my inspiration. Whether it is your first time reading my work, or you have been with me from my first novel, I thank you from the bottom of my heart for supporting me. I hope you will enjoy reading *Crossing Sisters* as much as I enjoyed writing it just for you.

Until the next novel,
Jessica Tilles
May 30, 2011, 2:10 p.m.
Home office, Upper Marlboro, Maryland
E-mail: Jessica@jessicatilles.com
Web site: www.jessicatilles.com

A NOTE FROM THE AUTHOR

Dear Reader:

This book took me over one year to write. I never take that long to write a book. I must admit, it was no easy task, as I had forgotten a lot of what I had written in the first book. Honestly, I did not want to crack open *In My Sisters' Corner* or even revisit the characters. But, when my readers make a request, I try my best to honor it.

In my Jessica Tilles fashion, I started the sequel days after the last chapter of *In My Sisters' Corner*. Therefore, if you are a first time reader of mine, I suggest you read *In My Sisters' Corner* first to eliminate any confusion. But, then again, I have a tendency of taking readers "back down memory lane."

Anyhow, I think you'll be quite pleased with the book you are holding in your hands, *Crossing Sisters*.

I do hope you will enjoy reading this book as much as I enjoyed writing it for you!

"*Sisters annoy, interfere, criticize. Indulge in monumental sulks, in huffs, in snide remarks. Borrow. Break. Monopolize the bathroom. Are always underfoot. But if catastrophe should strike, sisters are there. Defending you against all comers.*"
–Pam Brown

CHAPTER 1

Orlando, Florida, the Eve of the Funeral

With each passing moment, Maya grew disgusted as she stared at the back of China's nappy head. She looked psychotic. The one last nerve she had left, and her cuckoo of a sister was tap-dancing all over it like a bad version of Ginger Rogers and Fred Astaire! Watching her was like waiting for paint to dry—boring, annoying, and downright absurd! *One Who Flew Over the Cuckoo's Nest* is how Maya described China, looking like a patient fresh out of the asylum minus the straight jacket. Staring at a wall with disheveled hair was a true sign of depression.

Maya tilted her head and followed China's gaze to the crimson-colored walls. She wondered how anyone could sit and stare at a wall for hours, thinking China had always been a nut, yet everyone called her the crazy one. Still, despite it all, she felt sorry for her sister and all the pain she was enduring. However, Maya refused to mourn for Ron and didn't care for anyone else's opinion. She wasn't grieving the death of a pervert! He was a sick bastard who forced his children to watch pornography. As far as she was concerned, Ron should be burned to a crisp and his ashes flushed down the toilet with the rest of the shit.

Maya stretched her arms up high and leaned her head back. Followed by a soft moan, she lowered her arms and held her head straight, staring blandly across the room. Her stomach knotted around the ache in the pit of her stomach as she took an unforgettable trip down memory lane.

It was a chilly family weekend in Atlanta at the Howard's residence. Ember crackled under the dying fire in the black fireplace stove as the black private eye, John Shaft, hunted down the kidnapped daughter of a crime lord in the 1971 movie, *Shaft*. Sixteen-year-old Maya was sandwiched between China and Ron. Nestled in the corner of the sofa, China had missed most of the movie. The *itis* had set in after a large family dinner. China slept and her nastiness of a husband eyed the shapely legs of her teen-aged sister.

Barely out of puberty, Maya's thighs were hotter than the kitchen stove, and like a male dog sniffing around a bitch in heat, Ron knew it. She was no longer little Maya, but a young woman with junk in the trunk, a tight abdomen, and Betty Boop's tits.

Her denim cut-off shorts exposed silky smooth brown covered taut thighs, and Ron's dick was harder than Chinese Algebra.

She knew his perverted eyes were ogling her and she enjoyed every minute of it. She was young, dumb, and a huge flirt with absolutely no idea of the ramifications behind her actions.

Ron's breath reeked of the half-empty bottle of Jack Daniels sitting on the table in front of the sofa. The same table that held Maya's propped up foot.

A grin curled at the corner of his mouth. He leaned in and blew into her ear.

It tickled. She swatted at him. "Quit it!" she whispered.

He blew in her ear again.

The hair stood on the nape of her neck. She giggled.

He blew in her ear once again.

Her twat twitched, sending a slight chill throughout

her. It was a good throb that felt good to her, like nothing she'd ever felt before.

He reached for the bottle of booze and held it close to her lips. "Here," he said under his breath, "take a sip."

Without hesitation, she opened her lips.

He poured the warm spirit inside her mouth.

As she took in the liquid and allowed it to flow down the back of her throat, Ron's hand rubbed the soft flesh of her inner thigh and roamed up toward her crotch.

The fire was set ablaze, and Maya's thighs parted like the Red Sea.

Kissing his sixteen-year-old sister-in-law, Ron swiftly pulled Maya under him, pulling her thighs up to her chest. He eased his finger inside her virgin opening and wiggled it around, and her juvenile hips moved with his groove.

Without any guidance, she slipped her hand inside his sweat pants and moved down his abdomen, grabbing hold of him. An act she'd seen while watching *Porky's* on late-night television.

Turned on and excited beyond anything he'd ever felt before, he flicked and popped her little swollen knot, matched by her rapid hand strokes.

China watched as her husband ejaculated and her baby sister had her first orgasm.

Ron withdrew from the family room like a thief in the night and into the guest bedroom of his in-laws home that he shared with China.

Maya darted upstairs to her bedroom.

Her body trembled and a single teardrop fell down China's cheek. She was numb and beyond disgusted.

Why didn't she say anything? How could she just sit there and watch a grown man molest her teen-aged sister? As much as she wanted to say something, she couldn't. The knife piercing her heart stifled her cry. She heavily blinked as she didn't want to believe her eyes. However, the eyes don't lie. Realizing what had taken place before her, anger and hatred for Ron *and* Maya was like molten hot lava boiling to the top of a volcano ready to erupt and disintegrate all in its path. The devil inside her matched Ron's disgusting ass as she slowly rose from the couch and headed toward the bedroom, making a pit stop in the kitchen. She swiped the butcher's knife from the wooden block and crept into the guest bedroom.

Ron was out like a light.

You are one nasty motherfucker, she thought as she closed and locked the door behind her. He was going to pay for what he did to her sister.

Standing over him, she delicately separated his lips with her finger. His mouth opened. She slid the sharp blade of the butcher's knife inside his mouth until it touched the back of his throat.

He gagged.

"Don't you move," she snarled between clinched teeth.

The terrified look on his face was priceless and resembling something straight out of a *Chainsaw Massacre* movie.

"I saw what you did, you perverted bastard. I saw you, I saw you, I saw you! Calling the police and having your ass locked away behind bars is too good for you." She inched the blade in deeper. He heaved and gagged. "You need to die, you slimy son of a bitch." China seethed with anger and yet she was as cool as a cucumber.

Ron's body shook and heaved as tears ran down the side of his face. His eyes pleaded for his life.

"Give me your finger."

Ron didn't budge.

"What? You deaf? Give me your goddamn finger!"

Ron held up his left hand.

"Naw," she shook her head, "that ain't the hand you used to finger fuck my sister."

Reluctantly, Ron held up his middle finger.

China grabbed his finger and held it tightly.

Ron whimpered.

"Shut. The. Fuck. Up. You better not pant hard or else I'll cut out your fucking tongue. You understand me?"

Ron nodded his head.

With a crooked smile on her face, China pulled back Ron's finger, and Ron was panting like the dog that he was.

"What's wrong? Does it hurt the baby?" she said sarcastically as that smile on her face grew wider and wicked.

Quickly she pulled the blade out of his mouth and snapped his finger until it cracked.

Ron yelled and cried to the top of his lungs.

She smacked his broken finger and barked, "Bitch! The next time you look at my sister, I'll cut your dick off!"

Thunderous footsteps stormed down the stairs and throughout the house.

"China!" everyone called out. "What's wrong? Is everything alright in there?"

China looked at Ron. "Is everything alright?"

He didn't say a word.

China turned her back to him and unlocked the door. She looked over her shoulder and said, "Now your pain equals mine." She opened the door to see her sisters and parents. "Everything's fine. Ron just stumped his toe. Good night." She closed the door in their faces and locked it.

With the butcher's knife still in her hand, she pulled a pillow and the comforter off the bed and curled up in the wingback chair sitting in the corner of the room.

China never mentioned that night again and Ron took it to his grave. Maya figured China knew when she heard Ron's cry from whatever punishment China had laid on him, and prayed to God she did not encounter China's wrath, too.

It had been hours and China had not uttered one word since her sisters' arrival earlier that morning. In fact, she did not even open the door. After five minutes of constant doorbell ringing and knocking, Free tilted the oversized terracotta flowerpot that sat in the corner of the porch and felt around underneath for the spare key while Maya shifted her weight, huffing and puffing like a spoiled brat.

China took Ron's suicide extremely hard. She struggled with mixed feelings. Part of her wanted him dead because of all he had done to their children. She also wished she had been the one who pulled the trigger and watched that speeding bullet blow a powerful hole in the back of his head. Honestly, China would not have taken Ron's betrayal so hard had it not been for his indiscretions, leaving her to feel less than desirable and less than a woman. Every waking moment she sought answers to her questions as to why Ron desired the comfort of someone else. What was more frustrating was not having the answer to those questions, and since Ron committed such a cowardly act, her questions would remain unanswered. It was all disgusting as far as she was concerned, two men intertwined, rubbing, kissing, sucking, fucking...she would do everything in her power to ensure her son, Andre, does not end up like his daddy.

Agitated, Maya shifted around on the sofa, peering at her older sister. She was about to speak when Free entered the living room, stopping her short of hurling her usual venom of hatred at China, the sister she loved but could not stand.

"The dishes have been put away and I mopped the floor, too," said Free, smiling with her hands propped atop her full-figured hips. She looked at China and then to Maya where she held her gaze.

Maya shrugged her shoulders, rolled her eyes, and shook her head.

Free took a step closer to China and placed her hand on her shoulder. She noticed a tiny lint ball and picked it from her hair before speaking.

"China, honey, can I get you anything?"

China maintained her zombie-like state, so eerie and unlike her. In fact, it sent a spine tingling chill throughout Free. She was quite concerned that China may do something drastic, suicidal.

The need to say something was like a bad itch she needed to scratch and Maya could not hold her tongue to save her life. She was going to scratch that itch if it killed her.

"She's been sitting there for most of the day. I don't know what's wrong with her. She needs to–"

Free stood erect, squared her shoulders, and shot a piercing look at Maya, cutting her words short.

Maya tossed her hands up in the air. "What? Free…look at her! She hasn't moved." She folded her legs beneath her, Indian-style, and huffed. "It's kind of weird. Don't you think?"

Free sighed and sat in the recliner next to the marble fireplace, emblazoned with a hot ass fire in Orlando, Florida in the middle of July.

"She could've at least combed her hair," Maya insisted on pointing out. "And it's hot as shit in here! Who the hell lights a fire this time of year?"

Piling her micro braids atop her head, Free stretched her neck to the side and sighed from exhaustion. The drive from Atlanta had taken its toll on her, especially when Maya's lazy ass refused to drive.

She dabbed her forehead. *It is quite warm*, she thought before saying, "Leave her alone, Maya. You know she's dealing with something tragic."

"Has she bathed?"

"That's enough, Maya." Free spoke in her normal irritated tone often used when addressing Maya.

"For real, Free, it's not healthy." She sighed, looked at the fireplace and pulled her T-shirt over her head. "I think it is warm enough in here. Can we please douse that shit?"

Hissing, Free snapped her head toward Maya. "She's grieving," she snapped between clenched teeth. "What is wrong with you?"

Maya met Free's stare dead on. "What's wrong with me? You should ask her that question, a goddamn fire in the middle of July!" Not in the mood to go toe-to-toe with Free, the muscles in her face relaxed as her shoulders slouched. "It just breaks my heart. I wish there was something I could do." She dabbed the back of her neck with the T-shirt. "Damn, it's too hot in here, for real."

"Yes," Free released a slight chuckle, "it is warm. But I suppose China was cold, which–"

"No, China is crazy as shit!" Out of habit, Maya rubbed the twenty-something-year-old scar above her eye. "Just like when we were kids, she–"

Free's eyes rolled upward, her lips pursed. "Oh, let's not sing that same old song again, Maya. You were children and China didn't know any better."

"Yeah, well, I'll never forget it."

Although disheartening, it was no secret that China and Maya were not the best of friends. It may have had something to do with China lassoing Maya like a baby calf, pushing her down a flight of stairs when she was five years old, and leaving quite a nasty cut above her right eye for a lifetime of remembrance.

It was late 1970 and twelve-year-old China stood at the top of the stairs that led to a dark, damp, cold basement, surrounded by wood oak paneling. Knowing five-year-old Maya dreaded that horrid place and feared it immensely (from constant teasing about the Bogeyman and creepy crawly things that would eat her alive), she was determined to lock her away in hopes that maybe she would not be found. Maya was a spoiled brat that harbored all of Mama and Daddy's attention, and China felt neglected. *No one is going to miss her for a little while,* she thought, hunching her shoulders and crouching down, peering down the steps and into the darkness. The basement scared her, too, but she would never tell a soul.

She flipped the light switch and crept down the steps, careful not to make a sound, as if she would awaken a big, mean monster. She reached the bottom and looked down at the cold concrete floor until she spotted an extension cord coiled in the corner next to the monstrosity of a furnace. Instantly, she stood erect and her eyes widened close to the size of golf balls. She held her breath, balled her fists, and quickly darted over to the corner. She snatched up the extension cord and flew up the steps. Her feet were on fire.

At the top landing, she flipped off the light switch and started humming "You Are My Sunshine" as she trotted up the stairs toward the bedroom she shared with Maya and Jade. Since Free was the oldest, she had a room to herself.

China felt it was time for Maya to disappear. She loved her sister and did not want any real harm to come to her, but she was just sick of her for a hot minute.

China stood in the doorway with her legs crossed at the ankles, watching Maya as she played with her dolls. Her lips held the smirk of a demon seed. "Maya, you wanna play a game?"

"Yes," she shrieked, excited about playing with her big sister. Maya dropped her dolls and scurried over to China. "I wanna play!" A smile as wide as the Atlantic Ocean graced her angelic face.

"Well, come on then."

"Okay," Maya replied, taking one carpeted step at a time, holding tightly to the rail.

"Hurry up, Maya!"

"I'm comin," she said, finally descending the bottom step and running behind her big sister who held the trust of a five-year-old in her hands.

They ran through the living room and into the kitchen, stopping abruptly at the top of the stairs leading to the basement.

Maya's face reddened with fear. Her little body began to tremble. "Uh huh, China. I don't wanna go down dere. I scared."

"What are you scared of?" asked China, trying to coax her sister down the stairs so she could close the door behind her. She suppressed a slight chuckle.

"You said the Bogeyman was gon' get me, and I don't wanna go down dere." She started to cry.

China grabbed Maya by the arm, sat her sister down on the top step and sat down beside her. "Ain't no Bogeyman down there, you scaredy cat."

Maya was on the verge of wailing, nodding her head frantically, tears glistened her plump cheeks. "Uh huh."

"No, it's not." She took the extension cord and tied it around Maya's tiny ankles.

"Whatchu doing, China?"

"This gon' scare the Bogeyman. He won't hurt you with this 'round your ankles."

Maya was too young to know any better, looking at her sister with admiration and a huge smile. "Dats gon' scare him away?"

China nodded her head. "There," she said, tying the final knot in the extension cord. "You have to get up." China stood up and pulled Maya up with her. "Now stand right here. Okay?"

Maya looked up at China, eyes wide like a deer caught in headlights. The innocent soul was terrified beyond her imagination, fear blowing through her like a tornado and urine trickling down her tiny legs.

"I want Mommy," Maya cried out. "I want Mommy!" she cried out again, this time hollering at the top of her lungs.

Maya's high-pitched shrill angered China. "Stop crying, you big baby!" she snapped with anger, causing Maya to waiver. With not so much of a thought, China then yelled, "You get on my nerves!" and pushed little Maya down the wooden basement steps, slamming the door shut.

Loud, blood-curdling screams rose from the bowels of the basement up two levels to Free's bedroom where she was doing her homework. Startled, Free tossed her books to the floor and darted into the hallway. "What's wrong?" she yelled, looking into her sisters' bedroom. "Maya? China?" she called out, but no one responded.

The spine-tingling horrific screams continued as Free bolted down the steps toward the cries to see China standing with her back plastered against the basement door. A look of pleasure and contempt covered her face.

"What is going on, China?"

China remained quiet, never budging. Satisfaction pursed her lips.

"Mommy! Mommy!" came from behind the door, sending chills up and down Free's spine.

Free lunged toward China and shoved her to the side. "Girl, you better move out of my way!"

China stumbled to the side and slid against the wall, moving slowly toward the doorway of the kitchen.

"I didn't do anything," China whispered, fear now overcoming her as she realized Maya could be in serious danger.

Free flung the door open and flipped on the switch. "Maya?" Seeing her baby sister lying at the bottom of the step, in a fetal position, with blood oozing from her face, petrified her. "Call 911!" she yelled and ran down the steps. "What happened?" she asked, overwhelmed with tears. Her cry was deep, throaty, and pulled from deep within. "China, what did you do?"

China did not budge.

Free looked over her shoulder and yelled up into the kitchen with all of her might, "*Chiiiinnnnnaaaaaa*, call 911, *now!*"

China grabbed the phone and called 911. Her little knees knocked, for fear of being skinned alive.

Fortunately, Maya pulled through the ordeal with a permanent scar above the right eye and a temporary knot on the forehead.

China received the ass whipping of her life. The thin switch had instantly become an extension of her mother's right hand. Its swooshing sound whipped through the air blanketed the room before it connected with her tender brown skin.

"She's always messing with me, Mama!" she cried harder, her pleas ignored. When her mother's arm tired, the whipping ceased and China's ass was on fire. She was unable to sit down for hours. That was the end to China's attempts of getting rid of Maya. She simply had to learn to live with her.

Slowly, China turned her head toward Free and Maya. She stroked her tongue around the inside of her mouth. She was about to speak, but she paused in deep thought. She had not spoken in hours and her mouth felt dry and cottony. Lifting her hand, she raised her index finger and spoke above a whisper. "Don't talk," she paused as she cleared her throat, "about me as if I'm not here. That's rude."

Dramatically, Maya threw her hands up in the air in praise. "Hallelujah! The dead has arisen! We were getting worried about you, girl," Maya said sarcastically, reaching for the spring issue of *Spiegel* catalog on the small Mediterranean-style coffee table and flipping through the pages.

Stretching her legs out before her, China peered at Maya from the corner of her eye before addressing Free. "Thank you for cleaning the kitchen, Free. You've been a big help."

"I don't mind, China. That is why I'm here. Can I get you anything at all?"

"No, thank you." With the tips of her nails, China tapped the arm of the chair and looked around the massive living room. "What am I going to do now? I have no job and no husband."

Still flipping through the catalog, Maya confirmed, "You're going to continue living your life."

"I have no life," China rebutted.

"You know, China," Free started, "you could always open that hair salon you'd always talked about opening along with the restaurant."

Closing the catalog and returning it on the table, Maya chuckled. Then, she frowned up her face and immaturely sucked her teeth. "First of all, it sounds like something straight out of *BAPS*, and not with the way her head looks now. Besides, doesn't she need a cosmetology license or something?"

Free softly chuckled. Even though Maya was a huge agitator, there was truth in her words. China's head looked a hot mess.

"I could use something to drink, Free," chirped Maya, "since you're taking orders."

Free's facial expression spoke volumes. She snapped, "Do I look like your maid?"

"Well, no, but you did ask, and…oh, never mind." Unfolding her legs and stretching them out before her, Maya groaned, "I guess I'll get my own drink then," before standing and stretching her arms high above her head.

"Now that's a fine idea," Free warmly joked, smiling.

Maya smirked, turned up her nose and asked Free, "You want anything, smart ass?"

Free shook her head no.

"I'd like some water," China mumbled. "With cucumbers, please."

As her brows drew together in an agonized expression, Maya frowned at the thought of cucumbers floating in a glass of water. "Now that's some weird shit," Maya mumbled, disappearing into the kitchen.

China lovingly gazed at Free. She closed her eyes and vaguely smiled. The pain in her face matched the tears slowly creeping down her cheeks. Free remained calm and waited for China to speak. Free knew all too well what her sister was experiencing. Although she had never experienced the death of a spouse or significant other, losing both parents was no picnic. China's demeanor traveled Free to a place and time that saddened her tremendously where she never wanted to revisit. Her parents' funerals. For a moment, her heart felt heavy with a stinging in her eyes. She missed her parents, especially her mother. She would give her life to have her mother at her side. She shook it off and redirected her attention to China.

"Has anyone heard from Jade?"

China nodded her head. "Spoke with her yesterday."

"She is coming, isn't she?"

"She'll be here tonight. Flying in on Jon's private plane, *of course*."

"*Of course*! How did she get so damn lucky?" asked Maya, entering the living room. "You're out of cucumbers." Maya handed China the glass of water. "So, I used onions instead."

China looked at the glass of water, slowly rolled her eyes up toward Maya and snarled, "I should throw this shit in your face."

"She's back!" Maya chuckled, taking the glass of onion water from China. "I love you, too, and I'll get you a slice of lemon."

Free shook her head at Maya's comment. "So, what are we going to do tonight?"

"I don't know about you hens," Maya yelled from the kitchen, "but I'm going out tonight," she announced. "I'm feeling claustrophobic with Mother Theresa and Psycho Pattie."

China shook her head and looked at Free.

Returning China's look, Free smirked, shrugged her shoulders, and mouthed, "What are we going to do with her?"

"Put her up for adoption," China chuckled and Free fell out with laughter.

"Maya," Free yelled into the kitchen, "you need to keep your hot behind here. You're not in Kansas, Dorothy."

"You know, that actually sounds like a good idea," China admitted. "I haven't been out in years."

"Well then, let's go!" Maya squealed, entering the living room and handing China the glass of water with freshly sliced lemons.

"I don't know. Do you think it's a good idea to go out to a club on the eve of your husband's funeral?"

"He's dead, Free," countered Maya. "Do you think he's going to know?"

China stood up, wrapped her arms around her and arched her back. "Well, it wasn't a good idea that my husband fucked another man, but he did."

Free cringed with disgust and Maya's mouth fell opened.

"It wasn't a good idea that he forced our children to fondle each other," China continued, her tone now filled with anger, "but he made that happen, too." She faced Free. "So, forgive me if I don't give a shit about being disrespectful right now. I hope he's burning in hell with the devil's pitchfork poking at his faggot ass."

Pressing her hand against her chest, Free shook her head. "China, you don't mean that," said Free, studying China's face. The dark circles and lines forming at the creases of her eyes were telling of China's emotional state.

"Don't I?"

"No, you don't. I know how you're feeling, China, but–"

China's expression of anger turned to sarcasm. "Do you *really*, Free? How could you know how I feel? You still have your man."

"You're not the only one who has suffered a loss, and can we please not argue."

China ran her fingers through her matted hair and, for a quick minute, she, too, ventured down memory lane to the day her parents were buried. Out of all the sisters, Free took it the hardest.

"Yeah." She looked at Free and forced a smiled. "I know, sorry. Well," she paused and sighed, "I need to wash my hair."

Maya threw up her hands and sucked her teeth. "Oh no, I am not waiting for you to wash that head of yours. I'll catch y'all the next go-round."

"Fine," snapped China, but in a playful manner. "Take your hot ass on. We'll be fine." She looked at Free and smiled. "How about a movie?"

"I'll pop the popcorn," offered Free with glee. Watching movies was her favorite pastime.

"Good, and I'll make the Cosmopolitans."

"You'd better stay here with us, Maya," advised Free. "You'll have more fun!"

Maya smirked. "Maybe next time."

CHAPTER 2

Petite and cocoa tan, all eyes were on Maya as she strutted across the threshold of Breeze's Night Club. With her chin up and nose pointing upward, she knew she was turning heads of men and women. Her ego was in full bloom. The fullness of her firm, perfectly round bosom garnered most of the attention from potential male suitors. Her pearl-sized nipples beamed through the sheer, soft pink halter that hung loosely, resting around the hips of her snug Baby Phat jeans. From her short cropped 'do to her butterfly lashes, mesmerizing smile and cave-deep dimples, Maya diverted every inebriated testosterone from his drink of choice.

Small and quaint, with a cloud of smoke billowing overhead, Breeze's Night Club wasn't worth making too much noise over, but it was better than being cramped up in the house. Very different from the clubs in Los Angeles she had once frequented as a high-priced prostitute, but quite similar to those in Atlanta.

Maya looked around, taking in her surroundings. If the clientele looked the least bit sleazy, she would be out the door. So far, so good. Eyeing the bar, she spotted an empty stool. She maneuvered her way through the ocean of people across the small, crowded dance floor, adding a little pep in her step, bopping her head, and snapping her fingers to "Before I Let Go" by Frankie Beverly and Maze.

In order for her to grab that stool before anyone else, she had to squeeze through two men who were deep in conversation.

"Excuse me, please," she said, walking sideways between them and intoxicating their nostrils with the sweet smell of Haiku. She flashed an alluring smile at the one who immediately caught her attention. They locked eyes. "Pardon me," she flirted, rushing toward the barstool.

Admiring the small package with the voluptuous curves, he removed his attention from his friend, zeroed in on Maya's round behind, and watched it sway.

She knew he was watching. As Maya reached the bar, she raised her hip and climbed up on to the stool, securing a view of the dance floor. With the nod of her head, she motioned for the bartender.

"Riesling," she ordered, flashing a warming smile. "Please."

He returned her smile and tossed the white terrycloth bar towel over his shoulder, turning his back to retrieve a wine glass from the wooden rack extending down from the ceiling.

"Yo, man," said the brother to his friend whose eyes were glued to Maya's curvaceous figure. "Did you hear what I said?" His tongue was thick with his favorite spirit: Courvoisier VSOP.

The sound of irritation in his friend's voice snapped him back to reality. "Huh. Naw, I didn't catch it. What'd you say?"

"I asked if you will be joining us tomorrow on the course."

His attention quickly diverted back to Maya when he said, "Yeah. Yeah. Sure, I'll be there. What time?"

His friend followed his gaze and chuckled, clearly understanding why he did not have his friend's undivided attention. "Yeah, a'ight, man. Listen, tee time is at six sharp. Be there or be–"

With a pat on the arm, he abruptly dismissed his friend. "Let's chat later, man," he said, sitting his half-empty bottle of Corona with a slice of lime on the small table beside him before leaving his friend. He made his way over to the end of the bar where he had a clear view of her.

With closed eyes, a bobbing head, and snapping fingers, Maya's shoulders moved to James Brown's "The Big Payback." Feeling the rhythmic grooves, Maya's head snapped back when James bellowed, *"Hey, hey, hey!"*

He laughed, amused at her security, confidence, and the ability to be herself. He found those to be the most intriguing traits of any woman.

Maya was oblivious to her surroundings, not recognizing her admirer's fixated stare.

"One Riesling for the beautiful sister." The bartender sat the glass before her.

She opened her eyes and smiled. "Thank you," she sung out, throwing a flirtatious smile at the bartender. It had been a long minute since she had felt the comfort of a man. She desperately needed penetration and the bartender looked like a good candidate.

A tall lanky character eased up beside her, showcasing a row of tarnished gold teeth. "What's up, Lil' Mama?" He leaned down on the bar and moved in a little closer.

Maya leaned back and turned up her nose. He was a smoker. His breath smelled like hot shit.

He stroked her arm with his index finger as she flinched, pulling her arm closer to her body. "I see you all by yo self, pretty lady. You waitin' on somebody?"

She rolled her eyes upward, ignoring him.

Not having a clue, and ignoring her reluctance to converse, he persisted. "If I buy you a drink, can I sit here and talk to you?" He continued smiling broadly.

Sharply, she snapped her head to him and barked a stern, "No, thank you."

Realizing his persistency was not getting him anywhere, he moved along as he mumbled, "Trick," under his breath.

"Yo mama!" she retorted, loudly, making sure he heard her. "Stinky bastard," she mumbled as her glossy lips pressed against the rim of the glass, taking a sip.

That feeling of someone watching her invaded her senses, and it seemed as though everything on her began to itch, especially her nose. She hated when that happened. If someone was watching her, she surely could not scratch her nose. Her feminine instinct zeroed in on the target to her right and locked in. Like Samantha from Bewitched, she wrinkled her nose and thought, *let the games begin.*

After an hour of him turning down the likes of Halle Berry look-a-likes to the poorest looking tramps, few people he seemed to know, and hugging his drink, Maya's interest heightened.

Maya was working on her third glass of wine and ready to play his game, and play it well with every intention of winning.

Humph, he has no clue. Sweetheart, you are playing with fire!

She focused in on his long fingers, which made her tingle a bit. With her experience, a long index finger meant great clitoral stimulation and finger pleasing.

It was time to get the party started. Resting her elbow on the bar, she closed her eyes and ran her fingers through her hair, caressing the nape of her neck. Slow and seductively, she opened her eyes to meet his gaze.

Smiling, she parted her lips and seductively stroked her moist tongue across them, before she mouthed, "Hello."

He looked from side to side, then back at Maya. Grinning, he pointed to himself and mouthed, "Who me?"

She nodded, resting her elbow on the bar and raising her hand, turning her palm upward as she pointed her finger toward him and curled it back toward her, summoning him to her side.

His tall figure stood up, adjusted his jacket, and smoothly sauntered toward her. He was impeccably dressed in crisp cotton slacks with a very light shade of off-pink cotton, button down shirt. A man who can wear pink exudes confidence, and he wore it well.

With her back to him, he openly studied her. Looking over her shoulder and down toward the bar, he glanced at her ring finger. It was empty, not even a line. A smile graced his full lips.

Maya peered in the mirror at the handsome chocolate figure standing behind her. *Lawd have mercy on my soul. Whew!* Trying to ignore the calling from between her thighs, she crossed her legs and sipped her drink. *I feel a toothache coming on, he look so yummy.*

Through the mirror, their eyes locked and his nearness overwhelmed her. She caught her breath and she tried to maintain her composure.

Smiling widely, he exposed the prettiest row of teeth she had ever seen.

"Hello," he greeted in a deep, seductive voice that gave her spine tingling chills, causing the hair on her neck to stand. He pointed at the empty stool next to her. "Is this seat taken?"

Playing it cool, not wanting to show her nervousness, she nodded toward the stool and then turned her head in the opposite direction. She inhaled, bit down on her bottom lip, and exhaled slowly as she mumbled a tiny prayer. "Thank you, Jesus."

He caught glimpse of her expression and used that moment to admire the fullness of her bosom–38C, the perfect size–and curvature of her hips. Excitement stirring, feeling his johnson rise, he quickly took his seat.

The warmth of his hazel eyes seized.

"So, tell me," he said, smiling every so bashfully, "why isn't a beautiful woman at home tending to her man?" A whiff of his cologne was intoxicating and astounding her.

Looking toward him, she smirked, taking in every ounce of his delicious being. From his freshly manicured hands to his perfectly trimmed goatee surrounding the juiciest, fullest lips she had ever seen.

"If you were *my* man, please know that your every need would be tended to," is what she wanted to tell him, but instead, she asked, "Is that the best you've got?"

He projected an energy and power that undeniably turned her on. As much as she tried, she could not resist glancing at him in the mirror.

He chuckled at his corny line. "I thought I was giving you my best," he said, not letting on he was completely at a loss for words.

The smile in his eyes contained a sensuous flame, which made it hard for her to maintain her composure. She, too, was at a loss, but when it came to smart retorts, Maya was always on cue and this time was no different.

"Well if that's your best, sweetie, then I'd hate to see your worst."

Nodding in amusement at her quick wit and sense of humor, he held up a finger at the bartender. "I'll have a Corona," he said to the bartender. Then, he slightly turned his body toward her and said, "And the lady will have anything her heart desires," while he admired her beauty.

She chuckled and shook her head. "Okay, here we go, again." She adjusted her bottom on the stool. "So the bullshit begins to mount," she mumbled, trying to act like he was not having an effect on her. She refused to allow any man to see her sweat, and the heat that permeated from between her legs was making it very hard for her to remain cool, calm, and collected.

He smiled, before breaking into a deep, hearty chuckle.

"Um-hum, you had to laugh at that one yourself."

"Okay, I suppose those lines were a little lame." He extended his hand. "Reggie Hamilton, and I'm not the best at approaching such a beautiful woman."

She slipped her hand in his and smiled. His hand was soft and supple, definitely the hands of a pencil pusher.

"Keep working on it, I'm sure it'll get better. Maya Howard, it's nice to meet you, Mr. Hamilton."

He raised her hand to his lips and softly kissed her knuckles, holding it an extra few seconds. When she did not pull back, he relaxed his shoulders.

"So, Maya, what brings you out to Breeze's?"

Gently pulling back her hand, she brought the glass up to her lips. She pressed them against the rim and seductively sipped, stirring up the heat inside of him. She knew exactly what she was doing.

He flinched. *Damn! What is she trying to do to a brother, pulling out a page from the Female Player's Guide?*

"Well, *Reggie*, I'm here visiting my sister. Her husband committed suicide and his funeral is tomorrow."

He was not expecting such a response. "Wow, I'm sorry to hear that, Maya. Is there anything I can do?"

She looked at him amused. His sympathy was cute. "Thank you. I just needed to get out of the house. I have three sisters who all drive me crazy. And, my sister, China..." she paused before motioning with her hand, "her husband is the one who committed suicide...is on the verge of a nervous breakdown."

"I'm sure she is. It must be devastating for her."

Taking another seductive sip, she swallowed and then blew out a deep breath. "Yeah, I guess." For a moment, she pondered on his words. She supposed she would be devastated had she lost the man she loved too.

"So where do you fall?" he asked.

"What do you mean?"

"Are you the–"

"I'm the baby," she said, cutting his words short.

The DJ slowed it down a bit. The familiar opening piano melody of The Whisper's "Chocolate Girl" caused Maya to sway in her seat.

"Ooh," she cooed, "that's my song! I haven't heard that song in a long time." With closed eyes, she raised her arms in the air and snapped her fingers, her torso swaying from side to side.

Reggie took his cue, stood up and extended his hand. "May I?"

His move overwhelmed her, making her feel giddy inside. A feeling she had never felt before. She placed her hand in his and felt something electric. She slid off the barstool and he led them to the middle of the dance floor.

Slowly, he pulled her into an embrace, wrapping his arms around her waist as she naturally rested her head on his chest. His six-foot, two-hundred and twenty-five-pound muscular frame excited her. She closed her eyes and enjoyed the slow wind of his hips against hers. Instantly, everyone around them disappeared. Her feet left the floor as she felt like she was floating on a cloud. She inhaled deeply; he smelled good.

He leaned back a bit, holding firm to the small of her back. "You're a great dancer."

She looked up at him, gazed into his eyes and, for a moment, stared with longing for him. The hot tide of passion raged through both of them. An uneasy nervousness shot through her though, and it felt different yet unexplainable. It was strange for her. She never had a man to hold her as if she were as delicate as a flower. It felt nice. She felt special. His hand caressed the small of her back, his abdomen gently rotating against hers and the urge to sex him overwhelmed her. Partly due to his growing bulge.

His smile and seductive voice broke her trance. "A penny for your thoughts."

She broke their embrace and shook her head regretfully. "I'd better be going."

Confusion masked his face. "So soon? Was it something I said?"

"Of course not," she faintly smiled. "Early morning tomorrow," she nervously chuckled, "funeral and all. You know how it goes." *Oh, please ask for my number.* She wanted to see him again.

"Sure. I understand." His voice expressed disappointment, the muscles in his face relaxed into a frown.

He escorted her back to the bar. Pulling his wallet from his back pant pocket, he retrieved a business card and handed it to her. "I'm sure you'll be overwhelmed with family tomorrow. So, if you want to get away tomorrow night, give me a call. Maybe we could do dinner."

Taking the card, Maya smiled and said, "Thank you. I'll think about it. You have a good night." *Oh, I will definitely call you tomorrow.*

As she walked away, Reggie admired the wiggle in her hips.

I know he's looking at my ass. She looked over her shoulder and flashed a smile. *Um-hum, just as I thought, all up in my tail.* She giggled, pushing her way through the door.

CHAPTER 3

"Now you know," Free said, stuffing kernels of popped corn in her mouth, "I'm not into white men. But, if I were, I'd go after that George Clooney."

China chuckled, turning down the volume on the television. "Yeah, he is sexy."

"Uh huh," Free said, watching the rolling credits from *Ocean's Eleven*. "Brad Pitt ain't bad either."

"He's probably a dog, too."

"Not all men are dogs, China."

"He's alright. But I like me a dark chocolate man, so that Don Cheadle..." she paused, thinking about Ron's dark complexion. She choked back a tear.

"And?"

"And..." she paused again, pondering her next words. "That was a good movie. I hear it was based off the Rat Pack or something, you know, with Frank Sinatra and his crew." China slowly stood up like an eighty-year-old woman. Every bone in her body ached. She stretched her arms high above her head and yawned. "Whew! Do you want another drink?"

"Well, I don't know. It is getting late and we have to—"

China cut her eyes at Free with her lips twisted up in disgust.

"Okay, yeah," Free surrendered. "I'll have another."

"Good."

Free looked at her wristwatch and made note that Maya was still out. "I hope Maya is alright."

"She's fine. You know how that fast ass can be. Let her do her thing."

"I wish she would take charge of her life and stop living so recklessly."

China shook the silver cocktail shaker, poured the Cosmopolitan into the long-stemmed martini glasses, and took her seat beside her sister. "And whose fault do you think that is, honey?"

Free did not like the sound of that question. Free faced China and sat her glass down on the coffee table. She folded her hands tightly in her lap. "What exactly do you mean?"

"You took over the role of spoiling Maya when Mama and Daddy died. Instead of letting her grow up, you took her under your wing..." She paused to catch her breath. "Don't get me wrong, there's nothing wrong with taking her under your wing–"

"She *is* my sister, China," Free said with a ton of attitude. "She is *our* sister. And must I remind you that I did the same for *you* and Jade?"

Nodding, China took a sip of her drink. "You're right. And she's a grown ass woman now. If you continue coming to her aid, she'll never stand on her own two feet."

"That's what sisters are for. I'd do the same thing for you and Jade," she snapped, trying to control her anger. While she knew China's heart was in a good place, she was up to her eyeballs with being condemned about how she raised Maya.

China bit down on her bottom lip and massaged the back of her neck. "There's nothing I wouldn't do for my sisters. But–"

"Why do you hate Maya so much? What has she ever done to you?"

China remained quiet as she settled back into the sofa. Her face clouded with uneasiness. She sipped her Cosmopolitan before she spoke. "I don't *hate* my sister. That is such a strong word."

"Well, you seem to have some disdain toward her."

China rolled her eyes upward. "I don't hate her. I just don't like her."

"China, that's crazy. She's your sister."

"And I don't trust her."

Shaking her head, Free hissed at China. "You tell me what she has done to you."

"Let it go, Free. I really don't want to talk about it. I have enough to think about."

"Did she sleep with Ron or something? What did she do?"

"Please, can we just let it go?" China looked at the antique clock sitting on the fireplace mantel. It was ten-thirty. "Want to see another movie?"

Free jumped to her feet and propped her hands on her hips. "Not until you tell me, once and for all, why you hate our sister so much!"

"Yes!" she screamed before her voice drifted into a hushed whisper. "Yes. My sister fucked my husband." She peered up at Free and stood, not taking her eyes off her. She headed toward the stairs. "I hope you're satisfied. Now you know," she spoke over her shoulder, before disappearing up the stairs and into her room.

Free was speechless. Unable to move from the spot where she stood, her feet felt like they were dried in concrete. She swallowed hard and attempted to move. Her heart ached from China's words. *Of all the dirty*, she thought. She simply could not believe it. China had to have been mistaken. Free knew that Maya could be hot to trot, but never with her sister's husband.

Free willed her way up the stairs and stopped at the top landing, outside of China's master bedroom and stared at a closed door.

With short steps, she approached the door, rocking on the balls of her feet. She knocked. There was no answer.

"China, honey..." She tapped again. "May I come in?" Free did not wait for an answer. She wrapped her hand tightly around the doorknob, holding on for dear life. She held her breath and opened the door.

Seated on the edge of the bed, China had resumed her demonic stare, slightly rocking.

"Please, say it ain't so, China." A tear traveled down her cheek. "I just can't believe it."

"It's so." There was coldness and distance in her voice.

Moving closer to the bed, Free sat down beside China. "When? How?" She rested her hand on top of hers.

China pulled back her hand. "It was a long time ago."

Free wrung her hands, feeling uncomfortable, wishing she had never brought up the subject of Maya in the first place. Even when she was not around, Maya was a big pain in the ass.

China scooted back on the bed, kicked off her shoes, and leaned back against the headboard. She crossed her legs at the ankles and blankly looked at Free.

"Maya was sixteen. We were visiting Mama and Daddy's for the weekend. Jade had taken Ashley to see some Winnie the Pooh movie. I don't know where you were."

Free tilted her head to the side, trying to remember that weekend. Her memory was fuzzy.

China lowered her voice, being mysterious. "Everyone was asleep. Ron, Maya and I were watching a movie." She smiled. "*Shaft*—Ron's favorite movie. Anyway, I dozed off. When I woke up, Ron was on top of Maya, humping her like a dog in heat."

Free gasped, an overwhelming feeling of nausea soured her stomach. "What did you do?"

China surveyed the room, trying to suppress the tears. Her bottom lip trembled. Old memories compounded the continuous pain in her heart. "I said nothing. I didn't know what to say. I was shell shocked."

"You mean they were actually having sex in front of you?"

She sighed. "No dick penetration. He was finger fucking her and her little hips were moving like a little jack rabbit while she jerked him off."

Shaking her head, Free covered her face. "No visual needed."

"So, even though my sister stabbed me in the back, I still love her. She was young, although I want to believe she didn't know any better, but I knew better. She was just as hot in the ass then as she is now. Ron, on the other hand, knew what he was doing. A grown man playing with a little girl."

"Did you ever ask him about it?"

"Have you ever wondered why that middle finger always looked out of place?"

"Oh my God, you did that?"

She nodded, her bottom lip poked out. "I broke that bitch! He tried to blame her, saying it was her fault that he ended up on top of her. Said she teased him and was rubbing on his dick, and–"

Free cringed. "Penis."

"Dick. Piss stick. Rod. Member. Chocolate tool. Pile driver. Penetrator–"

Free pursed her lips; her face was without humor.

China fell out with laughter. "Stop being so frigid! You have a man. I know you're not a quiet fucker."

"That's my business, thank you very much! Did you ever talk to Maya about that night?"

"Nope."

"I think you should have talked to her instead of harboring such negative feelings all these years. That was nearly twenty years ago, China."

"I instantly hated her and didn't want to have a thing to do with her."

"Well, if you're not going to talk to her about it, then you need to pray on it, let go and let God, sister. All of this anger and hatred is killing our family. It must end and you're going to have to take the high road."

The front door slammed, diverting their attention.

"Hey, you bitches, guess what the cat drugged in?" yelled Maya from the front door.

"Where are my sisters?" Jade called out. "I'm here, I'm tired, and I want some of Free's cooking!"

"We'll be right down, Jade," Free called out before turning to China, and taking her by the hand. "It's time to let it go, honey.

Ron was sick and we know that. You can't blame a child who was taken advantage of by a grown man."

China smiled. "You're right, as always." They both stood and extended a warm, loving embrace. "I need to put the past behind me and move on with my life. Right?"

"Right," Free smiled.

They hugged again and walked arm-in-arm toward the bedroom door.

While walking down the stairs, with Free behind her, China yelled out to Maya, "I want to hear all about the club, you whore!"

Free popped her upside the head. "China, I thought—"

"It's going to take some time, geesh! You can't expect me to change overnight, can you?"

Free shook her head and they broke into laughter.

Jade and Maya looked on in curiosity.

CHAPTER 4

From the black leather handbag, China dumped the contents out onto the bed and lined up the mixture of MAC and Revlon cosmetics: eyeliner, rouge, pressed powder, lip glass and lipstick. Nerves wracked her being as she picked up the powder compact and opened the lid to expose the soft round sponge. Inhaling deeply, she raised her chin and stood sternly before the dresser mirror. As she patted the pressed powder over her face, paying close attention to the dark, puffy circles around and beneath her eyes, internally she cringed as she thought of that day's activities. Since Ron committed suicide, she had not had a good night's sleep. Shuttering as thoughts of Ron drifted back to the phone call she received from Marion, his lover, after she packed up Andre and Ashley in the middle of the night and drove from Orlando to Atlanta. China hissed away those thoughts.

"Packing it on a little thick, don't you think?" Jade chuckled, interrupting China's trip down a very haunting memory lane.

Ignoring her younger sister, China sucked her teeth, snapped the powder compact closed and tossed it on the bed.

"I need lipstick," she huffed.

Anxiety getting the best of her, she fumbled through the assortment of cosmetics and picked up the tube of Royal Red lipstick, stroking it across her full heart-shaped lips. She thought of her mother who loved Ruby Red lipstick. Chuckling to herself, she was the spitting image of her mother painting red across her lips. She, more than her siblings, resembled her mother the most. After pressing her lips together, she puckered in the mirror and dropped her hands to her side.

"You remind me of Mama," Jade reminisced. "She loved her red lipstick, too."

China smiled and looked at her sister. Their thoughts were always aligned.

"I sure wish I had Mama's strength," she sighed heavily, tossing her head back and sighing.

"How are you feeling, China? You haven't said much at all."

With closed eyes and with everything in her, she fought back the tears that she had been withholding since the call she received from Marion. How could she tell her sister that she could not find it in her heart to mourn the death of a man who had brought a gay man into their bed, let alone forced their children to act out scenes from pornography movies he kept hidden beneath the bed? She never knew him, that stranger who crawled in her bed, night after night for the last twenty years.

"I have nothing to say." She spoke sternly and well below a whisper.

China looked around the massive bedroom. She could still smell him. As much as she tried not to admit it, she truly missed her husband and loved him very much. Since his death, she slept in his flannel shirt. There was nothing special about the shirt. It was not his favorite. Nor was it hers. In fact, he hardly wore it. Still, wearing that shirt made her feel closer to a husband she loved so much, even though he was as deceitful as they come.

"I know this is hard for you, sis, but holding it in isn't good."

"What do you want me to say, Jade? My husband, the father of my children, is dead. He aimed a gun in his mouth and blew his brains out because he was ashamed of being gay and fucking up his children's heads."

It felt like she was on shaky ground. China walked backwards until her legs grazed the edge of the bed. She sat down and buried her face in her hands, crying tears of hate and resentment.

"I just wasn't enough for him," she sobbed.

Jade wrapped her arms around her sister and kissed her on the cheek. She desperately searched for the right words. She was truly at a loss. "I know how you feel, sweetie, it'll be–"

Quieting Jade with a raised hand, China broke their embrace. "No." She shook her head and waved her finger. "Don't tell me it's going to be alright." Her voice cracked as hot tears trickled over her round bronze-painted cheeks. She stood up and paced the floor. "Don't tell me you know how I feel either," she stopped pacing and faced Jade, "because that's a lie," she spewed at her with venom and pain. "*Why*," she cried emphasizing the word, "do people always say that?" She dropped her hands to her side and balled her fingers into fists. "You can't possibly know how I feel, Jade." She walked over to the dresser, and nervously rearranged items. "Don't, please don't do that to me…that 'you know how I feel' shit. I don't need to be coddled. My children have no father. I have no man. How can that be alright?" She leaned her weight against the dresser, folded her arms across her chest, and hung her head low. She tightly closed her eyes, took in a deep breath, and exhaled. "He could've come to me. We could've talked about it. We could've gotten help. I should've known my man was sick. How could I have not known my man was sick?" She faced Jade and softly said, "He was sick."

Pursing her lips and closing her eyes, Jade gently shook her head and remained quiet. Her heart ached for China and, not knowing what else to say, she quickly changed the subject.

"Where are my niece and nephew?"

"With friends."

"They're not going to the funeral?"

With a snap of the finger, her demeanor quickly changed, and China snapped, "Why should they? I can't say that I blame them. Shit, if I didn't have to go, I surely would not."

Speechless, Jade clasped her hands together and glared at China, gathering her thoughts. "It pains me to hear you speak with so much hate and disregard for your deceased husband. Yes, what Ron did was inexcusable, but harboring so much hatred isn't good for you or Ashley and Andre. Like you said, China, he was sick."

"Yep, he sure was one *sick* motherfucker. I'll tell you one thing," China barked, the tears dissipated and her hands affixed firmly to her curvy hips. "If he hadn't blown his brains out, I surely would have!"

"Oh, for goodness sake, China."

"Fuck that shit, Jade! I spent over $7,500 on a funeral. I should've had his ass cremated. He doesn't deserve to rest in peace!" she hollered to the top of her lungs.

Unable to digest what was being sad, Jade stood and headed for the door with China on her heels. "I'll see you downstairs."

"Yes, I'll see you downstairs," China snapped, slamming the door behind Jade, damn near knocking it off the hinges.

Extremely startled, Jade quickly faced the slammed door and opened her mouth to speak, but quickly changed her mind. She really did understand. Husband, mother, brother, father, sister, it does not matter. Losing someone you loved is never easy.

On the other side of the door with her hand tightly affixed to the doorknob, China dropped to her knees and prayed for forgiveness. Buried in her heart, she knew the deep-seeded anger she harbored was wrong, but she could not help it. She could not forgive Ron for what he did to their children and to her. Were the signs there? How could she have been so blind?

CHAPTER 5

Sharing a limousine with Jade, Maya, and Free was exactly what China had expected—annoying and nagging. The chill between the four lingered. Damn Ron for putting her through so much drama and turmoil.

"The service was nice, China," Jade commented. "The photo you chose of Ron was perfect."

"Yeah, I should've had an open casket, so people could see his no good perverted ass."

"Well," Free interjected, "it's a beautiful day today. Isn't it?"

"So much anger isn't good–"

"Yeah," China snapped, interrupting Jade, "how many times are you going to say that to me? When your man dies, you do things the way you want. Okay?"

Jade's eyes widened. The words fuck you lodged in her throat, realizing China was exerting her anger on those closest to her.

An eerie silence blanketed the inside of the limousine. A feeling of suffocation had taken over everyone.

As the limousine followed behind the hearse toward the cemetery, a flooding of hot exultant tears trickled down China's cheek. "Oh God," she whimpered, tears blinding and choking her.

The sisters all looked at each other. It was déjà vu. Internally, they each reminisced the day they buried their parents. For all of them, that day remained fresh in their hearts. If memory served Free correctly, the seating arrangement in the limousine was the same: China beside Free and Maya beside Jade. Free shivered at the thought and shrugged her shoulders, shaking it off.

Noticing, Jade asked, "Caught a chill?"

"Just a little," Free smiled. "I'm fine though."

Reaching into her purse, Maya pulled out a neatly wrapped joint and a lighter.

"Maya!" Free snapped, looking over her shoulder toward the front of the car, making sure the chauffeur's eyes were on the road. "Girl," she whispered between clinched teeth. "What are you doing? Put that away."

"I'm going to have me a smoke."

"Don't smoke that mess around me, please. It's illegal," Free huffed.

"Naw, it ain't illegal," Maya chuckled, taking the joint between her lips and lighting it. She inhaled deeply and held the smoke in the back of her throat as she said, "I have glaucoma!"

Laughter engulfed the car. However, Free found none of it funny. She was up to her eyeballs with Maya's shenanigans.

"Puff, puff, pass," said Jade.

Free's head snapped toward Jade. "You, too?"

"Well, this is an exception," Jade smiled. "But if Jon ever found out–"

"Dick whipped," Maya chirped.

"Yeah, Maya, hurry up and light that shit," China chimed in.

Jade rolled her eyes and gave Maya the finger. "Well, I ain't complaining. Jon does have some good dick."

"Jade!" Free exclaimed.

Jade giggled as she wrapped her glossed lips around the joint and drew long and hard.

Rolling down the window, Free stuck her face out like a puppy. "I don't want to get a connection from that mess."

Again, laughter erupted.

"*Contact*," Maya laughed as she took the joint from Jade. "You don't want to get a contact." She slipped the rolled stick between her lips, drawing heavily.

China dug down in her purse and pulled out a miniature bottle of Courvoisier V.S.O.P.

Free's eyes widened like a deer caught in blinding headlights. "You all are going straight to hell with gasoline drawers on!"

Jade opened the refrigerator and smiled from ear to ear. "Ah, my favorite! Grab those glasses by you, Free."

Reluctantly, Free distributed a glass to each one of her pot-smoking lush-head sisters. "This doesn't make any kind of sense," she huffed. "I swear you all act like adolescents."

"Thank you, honey," said Jade, taking the glass from Free. "I loves me some Dom Perignon."

"You're turning into a lush, Jade. You drink that stuff like its water." Free continued her fussing like the Mother Hen she truly was.

Inhaling deeply, Maya held the smoke in her throat as she spoke. "Well," she coughed, "that's some expensive ass water," she choked, coughing and gagging.

Free smirked at Maya's choking in amusement, and snapped, "Serves you right!"

"Stop hogging it, Maya," China ordered, tilting back her head as she took the contents of the miniature bottle down the back of her throat. The burning moving down the back of her throat eased her pain. Swallowing, she frowned up her face and released a loud, "Woo!" Then, she took the joint and pressed it between her red painted lips, drawing in long, deep, and hard. With her eyes closed, she held the smoke in her throat and leaned her head back against the seat, slowly swallowing and allowing the intoxicant to wrap tightly around her lungs, hoping it would take away all the painful feeling holding up hostage in her heart. "This is some good shit, Maya! Where'd you get it from?"

"Don't answer that!"

"Why not, Free?" Jade chuckled.

"Shot gun!" Maya yelled at China.

"Because I don't want to know! And it's illegal. I can't believe you all are smoking that mess out in public. It's going to get in all of our clothes. We can't go to the cemetery smelling like pot."

"We aren't in public and I told you it was for my glaucoma," Maya laughed. "Shot gun, China. Stop hogging it, damn!"

China flipped the joint and placed the lit end inside her mouth. Maya moved in close enough to be kissing sisters and drew in the smoke China blew out.

Free looked on in disgust because she never witnessed her sisters partaking in illegal activities. They all had completely lost their minds.

China watched as Maya leaned her head back against the seat and began chuckling. A feeling of depression had set in, but that was not supposed to have happened. Joints were supposed to make you happy, make you feel good, right? Why was she feeling like she wanted to put a razor blade to her wrist and watch the life drain out of her?

"I don't want to go," China interrupted, staring blankly out the window.

"Go where?" Free quizzed.

"To the cemetery."

"You have to go, honey," Jade consoled.

"No, I don't have to do shit but live and die!"

"China, you're being ridiculous," Free accused.

High as a kite, Maya jumped in. "It's that shit that's got her talking all crazy."

"Excuse me!" China yelled at the driver, but he could not hear her through the partition. Leaving her seat, she crawled across the floor of the limousine, between Free and Maya, and knocked on the partition. "Hello, damn it!"

As the partition rolled down, the driver looked in the rearview mirror.

"We don't want to go to the cemetery. Go somewhere else."

"I beg your pardon, Ma'am," he said with confusion.

"Beg for your own pardon and just do what I tell you to do."

Free hissed with embarrassment. "China, for goodness sake! How can you not go to your own husband's funeral?"

"He's already dead, he ain't gonna know if I'm there or not." Easing back in her seat, China frowned up her face and folded her arms across her chest like a spoiled, pouting five-year-old. "Damn it, I don't want to go to the fucking cemetery," she cried. "What's the big fucking deal? Damn! Damn! Damn!"

"Alright, China," Jade spoke softly. "We don't have to go." Looking up toward the front, Jade caught the driver's eye in the rearview. "Will you please take us back to the house, Robert?"

He nodded and raised the partition.

Maya contracted the non-stop giggles.

Free shook her head in disgust. "What about the hearse and the procession? We can't just pull out of the procession. We're leading it!"

Maya's giggling grew louder. "Ron's leading the procession!"

Jade shot Maya a look and then spoke to China. "Free is right, honey. You just can't "get out of line," so to speak."

"Damn! Damn! Damn, James!" yelled Maya followed by an outburst of laughter to wake the dead. "Y'all remember that episode?"

With a tilted head and turned up lip, China wiped away her tears and spoke to her sister in a calm manner. "You really shouldn't ride my back, Free. All of this here," she said, poking her finger in her chest, "is about me. It's not about you, dear sister. All my life, I lived for my husband and my children, never doing anything I wanted to do. I quit my job to be a housewife and burp babies that talk back, and all the while my husband was fucking men."

"What will people think if you don't show up at your own husband's funeral, China?"

"Fuck *people*, Free! I don't give a shit about *people*! That's the problem with this world. Everybody is so damn worried about *people*. Who the fuck is *people* anyway? *People* don't put food on my table, pay my mortgage, or put clothes on our backs. I'm so *fuckin'* sick of *people*, and their cousins, *they* and *everybody*. Who in the hell are *they* any damn way?"

Swallowing the sob that rose in her throat, Free looked at Jade and gently shook her head.

Jade contemplated how to cut through the tension that was as thick as a block of government cheese. She knew the perfect knife to slice through it.

Jade pulled her cell phone from her purse, pressed a key and said "Call Jon" into the mouthpiece.

All eyes were on Jade.

Jade smiled. "Y'all like my new toy? Jon gave it to me."

"I can't stand you, bitch," Maya chuckled. "Where can I find me a damn Jon?"

"You've had several," said China. "Seems like to me you'd had enough of them johns!" China laughed aloud, hysterically. Maya was always the butt of China's jokes.

Rolling her eyes at China, Maya extended her middle finger, kissed it and rolled her eyes.

"Back at you," China laughed.

Free hissed, annoyed. But what else was new? Her sisters agitated her to no end with all of their bickering and childish ways.

"Hi, sweetie," Jade sang above all the typical cutthroat words being passed around. "Things are fine, honey, how are you?" She paused and looked at China. "That's good. Listen, babe, I normally wouldn't ask this, but I would like to take my sisters shopping and... Oh, thank you! Yes, we will have a great time. I love you, too, and thanks again." Ending the call, Jade screeched like a wounded cat, but with pure excitement.

All eyes were on Jade.

"My sisters, *we* are about to hit the closest mall!"

"Now that's what I'm talking about," mellowed out Maya replied and so high, she was touching the sky with John Legend.

"This is not right. Not right at all," Free fussed. "China, I can't believe–"

"Let go and let God, Free," China retorted. "I'm going shopping and if Jon wants to pay for it–"

"You all are going straight to hell!" Free lashed out.

"And when was the last time your ass been inside of a church, Free? If I recall correctly, you're too busy fucking on Sunday mornings!" laughed Maya.

China and Jade fell out with laughter, and Free was so tight-lipped she looked like she had sucked on a lemon.

"Oh yeah," Maya continued. "Don't let Free's ass fool you. But I'll give her credit because she does praise the Lord when Sam is sticking it to her."

"Maya, you have a big mouth!" Free cried out with embarrassment.

"Yes, she certainly does," China sneered at Maya, "but we have to love her regardless of that big ass mouth."

Maya sucked her teeth, turned her head, and peered out the window. "Whatever, China."

Like a quiet storm, China revved up her mouth to lash out at Maya. Since Free was not fighting back, China was going to do it for her. "My HIV test was negative, what about yours, trick mama?"

"Oh God, China, not today," Jade pleaded. "That was below the belt. Can we *please* go shopping, spend Jon's money, and have a great day?"

China's spewed hatred cut Maya down to her core.

"Fuck you, China! My test came back negative, you bitch-married-to-a-down-low-fudge-packing-homo!"

"I can't stand it anymore!" Free said, knocking on the glass partition. "Pull over and let me out, please!"

"You know what, Maya?" China said calmly. "You have a lot of mouth. How much shit will you talk when I knock the shit out of you?"

"Come on, y'all. Damn, why is it that we can't be together longer than five minutes without being at each other's throats?" said Jade.

"Pull over the goddamn car!" Free screamed. "I'm speaking English, pull this bitch over. I can't take it any more of this bickering crap. I am done! You can kill each other for all care. Let me out of this fucking car!"

China, Maya, and Jade looked on in astonishment, surprised at Free's outburst and the vulgarity. It was completely out of her character.

As the car pulled over to the curb, Free flung the door open before the driver could make his way around to open it for her. "Y'all need counseling, Jesus, and more counseling!"

Following behind her, Jade called out, "Wait," as she crawled over China and out the car. "Free, where are you going?"

"I'm going back to Atlanta. I've had enough of this, Jade. I don't know why those two hate each other so much. I just don't understand it," she sobbed. "You and I are not ready to kill each other. They never have one kind word to say to each other and I'm just sick of it!"

Pulling her sister into a warm embrace, Jade stroked Free's back. "I know, honey, I know. China and Maya…well, they do love each other. They just have a strange way of showing it."

"No, that's not love," Free wept on Jade's shoulder. "Love is not an emotion, Jade, it's an action and they do not *act* like they love each other."

With one leg hanging out of the car, foot planted firmly on the curb, Maya leaned forward as her skirt inched up around her thick brown stocking-covered thigh. "Hey, bitches, are we going shopping or what?"

Ending their embrace, Jade looked at Free with a turned up smirk. "I think she was adopted," she chuckled.

"I heard that shit, Jade," Maya snapped, pulling her leg inside the car and scooting across the seat to the far side of the car. "Get in the car!"

Jade kissed Free on the cheek. "Let's go spend Jon's money."

"It's just not right."

Jade relaxed her shoulders. She was at the end of her rope with Free and her sisters. She understood and respected Free's values, but at the same time Free needed to know when to stand down and be quiet. Now was the time for her to exercise that option.

"Free, it's not your decision, honey," Jade said. "China is a grown woman. Let her be. Let her grieve in her own way. What you or I think at this point really doesn't matter. If there are going to be consequences based on China's actions, then she'll have to be the one to deal with them and we'll be there to support her. Stop pushing your beliefs and values on other people, sweetie. It's not cool."

Free was flabbergasted. "But I'm not–"

"It's all good," said Jade, tugging Free by the arm, pulling her toward the car. "Let's get our shop on."

CHAPTER 6

Surrounded by a sea of clothes racks, Maya stood in the full-length mirror at Macy's, modeling a short red number with exposed cleavage and a crotch-high slit.

"You look like a slut," Free teased.

Peering through the mirror at Free, Maya rolled her eyes and hissed between her teeth. "It takes one to know one."

"No, it takes *living with one* to know one," Free chuckled. "Now take off that prostitute gear."

With a raised brow, China glanced at Jade and smiled before breaking into hysterical laughter. "I love it, Free!"

Free leaned up against the entrance of the dressing room and folded her arms across her chest. "Dare I ask what it is you love, China?"

"Yeah, you're being real daring today with your smart ass mouth."

"And, might I add, that it is about damn time, too," Jade said. "I knew you would eventually get sick and tired of taking everyone else's smack."

"Yes, well, it's really not my persona and I don't like being this way. But you're right, I'm sick of being spoken to in any old kind of way. Disrespected, mistreated–"

"Oh, shut the fuck up, Free," Maya blurted, followed by laughter.

Jade walked over to Free, draped her arm around her shoulder, and kissed her on the cheek. "I couldn't agree with you more, dear sister." She cut her eyes at Maya and mouthed, "Behave."

Maya stuck out her tongue.

"Now, aren't you going to buy something?" Jade asked Free. "It's on Jon."

"And that's another thing, Jade." Free said, facing Jade with a motherly smirk. "Why would you take advantage of Jon's kindness and ask him to take us shopping?"

"Oh, there it goes. I knew that smart ass demeanor would revert, allowing the Queen Mother to come forth," China sneered.

Maya cleared her throat as she held up a hot pink halter dress, shorter than a tunic. "Excuse me. If you three hens are finished cackling–giving me a damn headache–Jade, I'll take this one."

As China sorted through the designer dresses, she looked over the rack and peered at Maya's taste in clothing. "What corner will be blessed with that ensemble?"

"The one in front of your damn house! You get on my goddamn nerves."

"Hush, Maya," Jade chastised, "all that damn cussing. Let's at least act like we have a shred of decorum."

"I'm ready to go," snapped Free. "I want to go home."

"Me too, I'm hungry," added China. "I'm sure there will be plenty of folks at the house with lots of food. You know how folks do at funerals."

"That's mighty grand of you, China, thinking people are going to bring food to your house when you didn't have the respect or decency to attend your husband's funeral. I swear, the class, if you ever had any, has gone clean out the window!"

China was fed up with the holier-than-thou attitude. Who did Free think she was? She wasn't any different from her sisters. "Free, why don't you take a damn enema and loosen up?"

"Okay, can we please get along? I'm taking us to dinner," Jade announced.

"You mean that rich motherfucker of yours is taking us to dinner," Maya's high ass replied.

Free sighed heavily, tossing her hands in the air. "I give up."

Jade threaded her arm through Free's arm. "I think that's a good idea. Our sisters are in a battle that we will never win." They both chuckled. "You've gotta love 'em."

Free leaned in and whispered in Jade's ear. "I don't have to do shit but live, go home, and fuck my man."

Jade's mouth flew open in astonishment. "Free! Oh my goodness, girl."

"You whisper too loud, Free," China chuckled, then instantly turning sad. "I wish I could say the same thing." Easing down in the hard-back, red-cushioned chair positioned next to the register, China buried her face in her hands and wept uncontrollably. "What did I do to make him not want me?"

With sorrow in their hearts, they looked solemnly at their sister, then at each other. Tears welled in their eyes, and each one cried for her. They felt helpless.

Free draped her purse over her shoulder and pointed toward Maya. "Jade, if you're going to buy that street walker dress for your sister, please do it so we can go. I'll take care of China. I think we need to go back to the house."

Maya extended her middle finger.

Jade smacked it down. "One day, somebody's gon' break your doggone finger."

CHAPTER 7

When the limousine arrived at China's palatial home, a slender, petite man dressed in black attire and dark shades stood on the front porch.

"I wonder who that could be," said China.

Maya rolled down the window. "Humph, whoever he is, he sure is small. But he's fine though."

"Slut," China whispered under her breath.

"Bitch," Maya returned.

"We need a cuss jar," snapped Free, "and a bar of soap. You all have the nastiest mouths I've ever heard. You definitely don't sound like ladies. Mama would be so displeased."

As they climbed out of the limousine and approached the front stoop, China smiled at the stranger standing at her front door with each sister flanked at her side.

China removed her shades. "Hi, may I help you?"

"Hello, China. It's good to finally meet you."

Recognizing the voice, China's smile instantly disappeared, her body stood erect. "What are you doing here? How dare you show your face?"

"I only want to pay my respects."

"Respect," China barked. "Respect? You condescending bastard! Get off my porch before I have your faggot ass arrested."

"Who is this, China?" Free asked, staring the stranger in his eyes, noticing the sadness hiding behind the forced smile.

"Yeah, China," Jade added. "Why don't you introduce us to your company?"

"He ain't no damn company, but since you asked, this is Marion."

Free extended her hand. "Nice to meet you, Marion. Please excuse my sister; I'm sure you can understand..."

China shot Free a nasty look. "You don't need to apologize for me. This is my damn house!"

Ignoring China, Free asked Marion, "Did you know Ron?"

"Oh yes," China snarled, "he knew Ron. He and Ron's asshole were best buddies."

Maya gasped and Free nearly passed out while Jade was cool, calm, collected and speechless.

"Now get the fuck off my stoop, you...you... I don't know what you are! Just want your ass off my property!"

Raising his head, Marion inhaled deeply and carefully contemplated a string of words to hurl at China. As bad as he wanted to invite her to his ass, he chose against it. Today, she buried her husband, the father of her children, and his lover. He understood her pain, but he was in pain, too. The man he loved killed himself, and he will never hear his voice, see his smile, or feel the intimacy of his touch again.

"I understand your being hostile toward me," he said, calmly. "However, I really do need to speak with you."

"Well I don't want *nor need* to speak with you!"

"It's important that I speak with you, China."

Free observed the concern in Marion's face and interjected. "China, hear him out. Hear what he has to say," she advised.

Snapping around, facing Free, China sneered like a rabid dog. And, between clinched teeth and tight lips, she made her point extremely clear. "I don't give a *good fuck* about what he has to say. Comprende, Ms. In-Everybody's-Damn-Business?" With the snap of her neck and the roll of her eyes, China turned her attention to her unwanted guest. "Now, if you don't get your raggedy ass off my porch, I will put a bullet so far up your ass, you'll be shitting out of your throat."

"Oh, for God's sake, China!" Jade blurted out. "Insane. Just simply insane."

"Well, Jade, I'll tell you what, honey, if you don't like any of what I have to say, then you can pack your shit and hop on the next thing smoking, baby, 'cause if I remember correctly, it wasn't too long ago that you were as disgustingly nasty..." she paused, looking at Marion, "as this here bitch. Except you were eating pussy and this nasty motherfucker sucks dicks. So, you can go to hell right along with his ass!"

"Wow," was all Maya could muster. Even for her, the hate-filled words spewing from China's mouth took her aback. China's behavior toward Marion was clearly unacceptable, but the anger and hostility regurgitated toward Jade was irreprehensible, hurtful, and across the line.

China whipped around and glared at Maya. "What?"

"I no speak-a-English," Maya said, backing down, clearly not a battle she wanted to fight. She had seen China's pissy side more times than she cared to remember, but there was something different about her today. The contempt she barked was the worst ever from China, especially toward Jade.

"Good," she barked, fumbling through her purse. "Where the fuck are my keys?" Feeling around the bottom of her purse, a well of emotions was building inside, soon to erupt like Mount Saint Helen. China's hot molten lava of emotions would burn everyone's ass if she did not find her keys quick. "Damn! Damn, double, damn!"

Jade reached out for her purse. "China, baby, let me help you."

She snatched away from Jade. "I don't need your help," China snapped angrily. She looked at Marion. "Why are you still here?"

Jade snatched the purse from China's grasp. "Well you're going to get my help, 'cause I've gotta pee!"

At that very moment, a calmness took over China as she relaxed her shoulders, tilted her head back, and released a loud shrill that would deafen the ears of any dog, startling everyone around her. "Why?" she cried out. "Why, dear God, why?"

Everyone felt helpless, even Marion.

Finding the key, Jade inserted it into the door. "Come inside, China." Jade escorted her by the elbow. "Come on, honey."

China fell into Jade's arms. Wanting to be strong, she tried to maintain for her children, but she could not do it any longer. An unbearable pain was what she felt, having lost her husband, lover, and best friend. Her spirit was broken and losing Ron caused it to shatter into a million little pieces. And, for her, she could not pick up those shattered pieces and glue them back together, even if she tried.

Free and Maya followed suit, closing the door on Marion.

CHAPTER 8

Once inside the house, Free darted to the living room and peered out the window as Marion slowly walked down the driveway. Curiosity was getting the best of her. What would he want with China? Fear shot through her as she thought the worse: AIDS. She bolted for the front door and called out to Marion.

"Please wait!" She yelled, fast-walking down the driveway. "Please. I don't know what's going on, but you said you needed to talk to my sister. Of course, she's in no mood to talk about anything, but if you would tell me what it is, I'll gladly give her the message."

"I really should speak with China, but since that probably won't happen…" he paused looking at her, noticing her look of sincerity. "I'm dying of AIDS." Marion could not be any more direct.

Free wavered, her eyes widening with concern. His words sent a shocking jolt through her. Words lodged in her throat, she felt like a deaf mute, unable to form words.

"Ron didn't know. I didn't have a chance before he…" His words trailed off as he gazed into Free's eyes looking for sympathy or any ounce of forgiveness. Instead, he saw fear. And, to his core, he knew it was not fear for him, but for her sister.

Still unable to speak, Free stood frozen. The thought of it all tore at her insides. Finally, she gasped. "Are you saying that my sister may have AIDS?" She shook her head in denial. "No, that can't be. In fact, today she said her test came back negative."

"She should be tested again in three months. She should be tested regularly every six months. I'll pray she hasn't been infected."

"Do you–" Interrupted by the dryness in her throat, she cleared it and swallowed hard. "Do you think Ron may have been…" she paused, looking around as if she was about to utter vulgarity and didn't want anyone else to hear, "…infected?"

"I don't know."

"How long had you two been…uh…um…?" She looked away from him. She could not believe she was having this conversation.

"Seeing each other?" he added.

She shook her head with a forced smile, uncomfortable with the topic of discussion. She was not homophobic. On the contrary, she did not care what people did behind their closed doors, so long as they did not force their beliefs on her.

"Please forgive me, this is very awkward for me," she said, picturing Marion and Ron intertwined in some nasty hotel, performing intimates acts that should only be shared between a man and woman. It disgusted her to her very being. She shivered, shaking off the nauseated feeling. She thought she would throw up any minute.

Marion nodded his understanding and continued. "A little over a year, but," he quickly added, "I have to tell you that I didn't know he was married until recently. Like China, I felt betrayed, but I loved him."

Instantly, her stomach clenched into a tight ball of muscle. She desperately wanted to retreat from the encounter she had brought upon herself.

"Well, I'll have a talk with China. I suppose it would be better coming from me than–" she stopped short and peered at Marion. "you." A hint of sarcasm sprinkled her voice.

Ignoring her snide remark, Marion grabbed Free's hand and thanked her. She cringed as their flesh connected. His hand was cold and clammy, yet soft and supple. Although she wasn't ignorant to the disease, there was still something about being so close to someone who was dying, right before her eyes, that made her feel icky. She wanted to bathe the day away.

"You're welcome," she managed to say. She looked away, gathering her words, trying hard not to be offensive. "Uh, may I ask you how long you have?"

"Six months, maybe a year…"

A lump formed in her throat, and without warning, tears flowed like the River Nile down her cheeks. She felt awful for Marion. She did not know Marion from Adam, but he looked so young. Too young to be dying.

Why don't these people use protection?

"I don't understand," he said. "We were always careful. I mean, especially me. I always insisted Ron wore a condom."

Squaring her shoulders, she all of a sudden became offended and protective over her brother-in-law. "So, you had an affair on Ron. Is that how you got it?"

His eyes narrowed and his back became ramrod straight. "No. I was faithful to Ron. He cheated on me. Obviously, I wasn't enough for him."

Free closed her eyes as Marion's words echoed China's. "Wow," she whispered. "Just when you think you know someone…" She peered at Marion. She could understand Ron's attraction to him for he was a very attractive man. Nothing about him looked feminine. He was as masculine as a defensive lineman, yet small. But, then again, she had heard about those in-the-closet athletes. "Just when…I suppose none of us knew him at all."

With that said, Free turned on her heels and hurried to the front door, where she wrapped her hand around the doorknob and looked back over hear shoulder at Marion. He peered at her with dark, helpless eyes. She briefly closed her eyes, said a quick prayer and went inside the house.

Jade was peering out the window, watching Marion walk in a slow gait. "What was that all about?"

Free shook her head. "Just unbelievable."

"What is unbelievable? What did he say?"

Grabbing Jade by the arm, steadying herself, she whispered, "He said he has AIDS."

Jade took a deep breath and held it. Placing her hand on her chest, she slowly exhaled and grabbed her forehead. "AIDS? Oh, dear God," she whispered. She looked into her sister's eyes with fear. "Free, are you saying–"

"We need to talk to China."

CHAPTER 9

As China predicted, swarms of people embarked on her home carrying homemade dishes of macaroni and cheese, collard greens, fried chicken, candied yams, a whole turkey, whole hams, homemade rolls, potato salad, cakes, pies, bags of ice, and cases of sodas. Surprisingly, no one questioned her lack of appearance at Ron's funeral.

Until the last guest left, Free contemplated how she would disclose the details of her conversation with Marion. She had been holding what she had learned for hours, just eating her up on the inside. Free didn't know the first thing about AIDS, other than contracting it from having sex and through using dirty needles, or possibly a blood transfusion, but that was about it. Because she kept close to home and focused on her business, Free was ignorant to the outside world and all of its issues. Moreover, all of this made her think about her sexual relations with Sam. As far as she could remember, they had only used a condom once and that was their first time. But, from that point on, they were bare backing every chance they got.

Damn it!

Fear for her safety pounced on her chest.

Sam wasn't sexually active before we met. In fact, he was celibate. That thought eased her mind some.

"Thank you for coming," China said, closing the door behind the last of the lingerers. She leaned her back against the door. "Whew, I'm tired. We have so much food. I'll bag it up and freeze it."

Jade looked over at Free and then back at China.

Free nodded at Jade and spoke softly to China. "Honey, we need to talk."

"Girl, those collard greens melted in your mouth, and that ham… I think I'm going to fix myself a third helping," China half laughed, trying to hold back the pain from the day's activities.

"There's enough food to last us a good little while. Free, you make sure you take one of those hams back to Atlanta with you. I'm not going to eat three hams, that's for sure."

"China?" Jade echoed Free and said, quite calmly, "Honey, we need to talk to you."

Wearing a hot pink hoochie ensemble, compliments of Jon Meadows, Maya trotted down the steps and posed before her sisters. "Well? How do I look?"

"Like a fashion emergency," China responded. "Well, at least you'll be the best dressed hooker on the corner." China fell out with laughter and walked into the kitchen. "I crack myself up."

Catching Jade's eye, Maya held her tongue and followed them into the kitchen.

"China, honey, we really need to speak with you," Free reiterated. "It's very important."

China looked around the kitchen. "I think I'm going to do what I've always wanted to do and paint the kitchen yellow! Ron always stood in my way when I wanted to paint the kitchen, but there ain't nothing he can say about it now, is there?" she laughed, humoring herself again as she looked down at the floor. "Could stand a new floor, too." She propped her hands on her hips and spun around, until she faced her sisters. "You know what I'm going to do, y'all?"

They shook their heads, looked at her, and smiled blandly.

"I'm going to sell the house! Yep, that's what I'll do. It is too big any damn way. Hey, I can move to *Hot*lanta with you and Maya, Free. Yeah, I'll move back home. There's nothing here for me."

"That sounds nice, honey. I think you should do whatever you want to do," said Jade, looking at Free, and then back at China. "However, we really want to speak with you. It's important."

"Let's see…" Folding her arms across her chest, she grew silent as if in deep thought. Then, she shook her finger and declared, "I'll call the realtor in the morning. There's quite a bit of equity in the house since we've never taken out a home equity loan. You know, Ron was so–"

"China, please!" Free exclaimed. "Just give us one minute of your time, please!"

The urgency in Free's voice moved China over to the table where she pulled out a chair and took a seat. "What's wrong?" She looked from China to Jade and then at Maya. "What is it?"

Jade and Free followed suit and sat at the kitchen table across from China. Maya stood up against the kitchen counter curious to know what was going on, too.

"Honey," Free began, reaching across the table to take China's hand in hers, "I don't know how to say this, but–"

China snatched her hand from Free's grasp. "Just say it."

Jade blurted out, "Free had a talk with Marion."

China's head snapped from Jade to Free, and slightly tilted to the side. "Oh?"

Clearing her throat, and once again, Free took China's hand in hers and forced out the words, "Marion has AIDS."

China withdrew her hand, relaxed her shoulders and sat in silence, staring through Free as if she were a plate glass window. After a couple of minutes, she broke through the cloud of silence hovering overhead. "I was tested for HIV and I am negative."

"You have to get tested again, China," Maya chimed in, standing in the doorway of the kitchen.

"Yes, I know. I go back in three months."

"China, he says he's dying. I asked him if–"

"I don't want to hear any more, Free. Thank you for telling me, but Ron is dead. I've been tested and I'm fine. I just want to go on with my life and do what I need to do for Ashley and Andre."

"Of course," Free said, forcing a smile, "and we are here for you." She looked at Maya and Jade. "Right, sisters?"

"Right!" they responded in unison.

"Great! Anyone for cake and ice cream?"

"None for me," said Maya. "So, if you Golden Girls will excuse me, I have a call to make."

CHAPTER 10

Maya sat quietly on the bed, biting down on her bottom lip. She read the business card and dialed the number. She pressed the phone firmly against her ear while tapping her bare foot against the cool hardwood floor. Why was she so nervous? It was not as if she had never talked to a man before. Yet, this felt different. Those same stirring feelings she felt at Breeze's Night Club never left her. She felt giddy and excited about him, almost like a little girl. As the phone continued to ring for the third time, she read the card: Reggie Hamilton, Attorney-at-Law.

"Reggie Hamilton," he answered on the fourth ring.

"Why so formal?"

He did not recognize the voice. "Who's calling?"

"This is Maya. You and I met last night at the club."

"Yes, I remember."

She could hear the wide smile in his voice.

He cleared his throat, out of nervousness, and continued. "How was the funeral?"

"It was a funeral. You know how funerals go."

Reggie sat down on the Italian leather sofa, stretched his legs out before him, crossing them at the ankles and trying to relax.

"So, Maya, I'm hoping you're calling to take me up on my dinner invitation."

"Well, I'm not hungry. Everyone brought gobs of food. You know how it goes."

"Yes, I know what you mean." He sat up and rested his elbows on his knees. He was becoming annoyed with himself. He had never been speechless when it came to women, always the one to initiate the conversation. But right now, he was a loss for words. He felt like a death mute and could not form words if you paid him.

"Can I come over?" She silently gasped at the words that fluidly escaped her mouth. Being forward had never been an issue until now. Reggie seemed to be a different caliber of man and she did not want to mess things up. She surely did not want him to think she was a fast tail. Truth be told, her ass was hotter than a firecracker on the Fourth of July.

"Sure. You're not one of those stalkers, are you?"

"No, silly, I'm not," she chuckled lightly.

He smiled. "10 Orange Drive. Write it down."

"Well, I don't have a car and I'm not from Orlando. I live in Atlanta."

"I suppose I could come and pick you up," he offered.

"Oh, yeah, I guess..." She briefly pondered his offer. The house was filled with too much emotion and grief, and Maya was not ready for her sisters to meet a man she did not know a thing about. Besides, Free would have a heart attack. Then, she thought about Robert. "Wait. I have your address. I'll find you."

"Are you sure?"

"Yes, I'm sure."

"Do you promise?"

"Do I promise what?"

"That you'll find me."

"I already have found you. See you soon," she said, making a faint kissing sound over the phone, before hanging up.

Reggie looked at the phone and smiled. *Did she blow me a kiss?* Of course, and he thought it was the sweetest gesture from a stranger.

Maya was beyond excited! She danced around the room, snapping her fingers and contemplating what she was going to wear. She only packed for a few days and she could not wear what she wore to the club the night before. She faced the mirror and admired the dress. She wondered if the dress was too much. She chuckled. China was right. She does look like a two-cent slut. What was she thinking when she picked out that little hot number? Her gut told her Reggie was different and she wanted to put her best foot forward.

There was a soft knock at the door.

"Come on in, Jade."

The door slowly opened. "How did you know it was me?"

"Because you're the only one who isn't rude and knocks before entering."

Jade walked into the guest bedroom and sat down on the bed. She watched Maya as she posed before the oval, mahogany encased floor-length mirror.

Maya saw Jade's image peering at her through the mirror. She turned around and snapped, "What?"

"You really do look like a slut in that dress."

"Shut the hell up!" She smiled and shook her head. "It's the truth though!" Maya admitted. She flopped down on the bed beside Jade. "I need a favor, please."

"Sure, anything."

"May I borrow Robert tonight?"

"Not again, Maya. Didn't you learn from the last time you try to hump him?"

"No! I'm not talking about that, Jade. Dang, don't you ever forget shit?"

"No, I don't."

How could she forget? It was the most embarrassing moment of Jade's life. A few weeks ago, prior to Ron's suicide, at the impromptu sister reunion at Free's home, Maya's lips were like a suction cup on Robert's dick in the back of a black limousine. A man Maya had only known for five minutes. To make matters worse, she was witnessed by Ashley, China's twelve-year-old daughter. From there, it was all a disgusting mess as Ashley mimicked her Auntie Maya, trying to perform oral sex on her ten-year-old brother. No, she would never forget for all the tea in China.

"Well, I have a date tonight and I need Robert to drive me."

Jade leaned back and stared at Maya in amazement. "A date? With who?"

"Well, his name is Reggie and I met him–"

"Reggie? What kind of name is that?"

"It sounds regal, don't it?"

"Doesn't it," she corrected, "and it's another word for black." Jade folded her arms across her chest. "So why do you need Robert?"

"Because I don't know this guy and I would feel safe knowing Robert was outside, at least."

"Okay, but Robert is not here, Maya. He's at his hotel. I don't think we should call him to come take you on a date. Why can't this Reggie person pick you up?"

"Because, Jade, I don't want to hear China and Free's mouths. You know how they are."

"That's nonsense. If he were any kind of man, he would come and pick you up. You know what Mama used to say: 'We don't drive to men, they drive to us.'"

Maya sighed heavily, sick and tired of everyone telling her what to do. Always being lectured to, it drove her up every wall in the house.

"You know, just once I would like for someone to be on my side. I'm so sick–"

"What? I'm not on your side because I will not let you bother Robert?"

"Just forget it, Jade. I'll take a damn cab."

"Maya, China has two cars in the driveway. I'm sure she will let you drive one of them."

"Yeah, I'll ask her," she mumbled, knowing China would probably say no, just to be her usual wicked bitchy ass self.

Maya took one last look in the full-length mirror and posed. "How do I look," she asked Jade.

"Well, you look like you could be bought really cheap," is what Jade wanted to say, but instead she said, "You look beautiful, sis. Just be careful."

CHAPTER 11

With her hand affixed to the doorknob, Maya puckered up her glossed lips and blew her sisters a kiss goodbye before she swiped the keys to China's black 2004 Volvo S60 from the foyer table. She opened the door and skipped outside to the tune of Mary J. Blige's "Real Love" bopping around in her head. She got as far as the top step of the porch when she stopped, peered up at the deep black sky, inhaled, and made a wish. She would have wished on a dog crossing the street if it would guarantee her a good lay tonight. She swung her Gucci bag over her shoulder and, with the palms of her hands, smoothed her dress, caressed the curve of her hips, followed by a pat on her hefty booty. Feeling giddy and tingling all over, she said a little prayer, "Lord, please let me get some tonight," before descending the steps toward the car.

Unlocking the car and opening the driver's door, she tossed her bag on the passenger seat. She slid her fingers down her chest and into her bra where she kept Reggie's address for safekeeping. She turned the ignition switch for she was eager to type his address into the GPS. This GPS stuff was all new to her, so she pushed every wrong button before pressing the right button to enter the address. After entering the address, she fastened her seatbelt, adjusted the rearview mirror, and exhaled.

Here we go!

She put the car into reverse, carefully backing out of China's winding driveway and into the middle of the street. She then shifted into drive and headed westbound.

"AT THE LIGHT, TURN RIGHT," the female voice of the GPS with the Australian accent announced.

Idling at the light, Maya turned on the CD player and could not believe her ears. "What in the world…is that Lee Ann Rimes or some shit? No wait, that's the American Idol chick, Carrie something. Well, I'll be damned. I had no idea China liked…uh, country."

"AT THE NEXT LIGHT, TURN LEFT."

"Okay, the light just turned green, I'm turning," she fussed.

After turning left, she proceeded down the street as she listened for the next set of directions.

"AT THE NEXT LIGHT, TURN LEFT."

Maya did not have a clue where she was going, but she trusted the GPS not to get her lost.

"DRIVE ONE-FOURTH MILE AND TURN RIGHT."

Turning right, Maya came upon a community of expensive looking homes with Spanish stucco exteriors that reminded her so much of Los Angeles.

"AT THE STOP SIGN, TURN RIGHT. YOUR DESTINATION IS ON THE LEFT."

Driving slowly, Maya could not believe her eyes.

Jackpot!

The palatial estate was breathtaking. Although it was dark, the full moon was the backdrop. She rummaged through the bottom of her purse for her cell phone to call her sisters.

China answered on the second ring. "Hello?"

Maya also heard Free and Jade in the background, sounding like cackling hens. "China, it's me."

"What's up, me?"

"Girl, you won't believe this. I think I done struck gold."

"What are you talking about?"

"Put me on speaker, I want Jade and Free to hear, too."

China pressed the intercom button and gently placed the receiver in its cradle. "Okay, can you hear me?"

"Yeah, can y'all hear me?"

"No, I'm deaf," snapped China, jokingly. "Now what is it?"

"What about Jade and Free, can they–"

"Maya!" shouted China.

"Okay, just wanted to make sure y'all can hear me."

"Damn, we can hear now what the hell is it?"

She heard Free giggling in the background. She also heard Jade adding, "That girl is too much," followed by delicate chuckling.

"Anyway," Maya started. "Check this out. I think I met me a Jon, Jade. Homeboy lives in a luxury estate home on a cul-de-sac with a rock waterfall and fountains and shit. The lawn is meticulous, and..." she paused, grabbing her bag and keys as she climbed out of the car.

"Where is my car, Maya?"

"I'm not answering that dumb ass question, China."

"Just making sure you haven't wrecked my shit. It's not paid off yet."

Maya heard Free and Jade giggling in the background.

"So, he has money, huh, Maya?" asked Jade.

"Either that or he's the damn butler," Maya retorted.

"Finish telling us–"

"Oh shit!" she exclaimed, cutting off Free.

"What's wrong? What you do, run my damn car into something?"

"No, China, damn! You should see this shit. The Hummer, Mercedes and Jaguar in the damn three-car garage."

"That sounds expensive, Maya," said Jade.

"Have a good time and be safe," said Free.

"Keep your goddamn legs closed, you slut," added China.

"Kiss my ass," Maya barked.

"Seriously, don't fuck him. Let his ass wait, shit."

"Okay, China, will do," she lied. If he offered up his dick on a silver platter, she was definitely going to taste it. "I'll call y'all back after I get inside."

China laughed. "Um, we'll be waiting with bated breath." She looked at Jade and Maya, declaring, "She's going to fuck him."

"Well, of course," Jade laughed. "That's Maya!"

"Clap booty," Free said, with a smirk. Surprised by her comment, China and Jade peered at Free. "What? What's wrong with y'all?"

They all fell out with laughter.

"All of y'all can go straight to hell," she snapped and closed her phone.

As she walked up the cobblestone driveway, being careful not to get her heel stuck in the cracks, the butterflies fluttered around in Maya's stomach. She was nervous, anxious, and excited—feelings that were balled up in the pit of her stomach like a tight muscle—by the time she reached the front door. So excited, she had to pee.

Maya rang the doorbell.

When he opened the door, the wafting of his cologne arrested her senses, causing a twitch between her thighs.

Damn, I forgot to put on panties! Yeah right! If she forgot, then the Pope is Hispanic.

"Welcome to my home, Maya." He greeted her with a wide smile that exposed his pearly whites and delectable, thick lips.

"Um, hey..."

Unable to move, Maya's feet were like concrete blocks, heavy with each step that she tried taking. *Damn it, Maya, girl, get your composure.* She straightened her back and squared her shoulders.

"It's good to see you again, Reggie." She walked past him and into the openness of the foyer.

Good googa mooga! She turned around in circles like a dog chasing his tail, but only in slow motion.

"You have a beautiful home."

He smiled at her. "Thank you." He made a lustful stare at her; however, he was not sure whether she was impressed or completely shocked.

Reggie then made a slight chuckle, thinking, *I can smell her sweetness already. I will definitely tap that ass in just a…*

"Well, take me on a tour," she said, interrupting his thoughts and warming up to him.

"Alright." He pointed to his left. "Here is the living room." He pointed ahead of them. "Adjacent the living room is the dining room."

As they moved through the living room, they stepped down into the dining room where she faced floor-to-ceiling windows. She just about fainted when she spotted the Olympic-sized swimming pool, spa and rock waterfall, and fountains overlooking a panoramic view of a manmade lake. The first floor to his place was richly decorated with custom wall accents, a gourmet kitchen with a butler's pantry, expensive crown molding, and Crèma Marfil marble. The staircase and much of the second floor was cherry wood. By the time they made it to the master bedroom, Maya stood dumbfounded in front of the custom-built closets. It was like standing inside a mini department store. His tailor-made suits hung flawlessly across from the cotton and silk shirts organized by color and fabric. Silk ties hung on a round movable tie rack.

"Well, this is my humble abode."

There ain't nothing humble about this shit. Damn, look at that bed.

"Would you care for a glass of wine?" he asked, taking note of her sculptured legs in the shape of a Coke bottle. He appeared to have drifted deep in thought. *I would love to have those wrapped around my…*

"May I use your bathroom?" she asked, interrupting his *Real Sex* moment. The heat between her thighs had reached an all-time high and she needed to freshen up.

"Sure," he pointed to a door. "It's right there."

She made a slow pivot and smiled, giving him that don't-you-go-anywhere look and switched across the room.

Inside the bathroom, she locked the door, dug into her bag, and pulled out her cell. She had to call her sisters.

China answered on the first ring. "Took you long enough! You're on speaker."

She spoke barely above a whisper. "Oh my God!"

"It's all of that, huh?" asked Jade.

"Girl, you have no idea," Maya replied. "Okay, Jade, how do I deal with a rich man?"

"The same way you would deal with a broke ass man," China chimed in.

"That's right," said Jade. "The money doesn't make the man, girl, do your thing."

Maya joked, "So, I can fuck him, 'cause I sure am horny. And he is one beautiful man."

"You are such the whore," China snapped, ending the call.

Maya folded her phone and dropped it inside her bag. She then peered at her reflection in the bronze beveled mirror. Assessing her makeup, all was well but the moisture between her legs had become overwhelming. She had never produced that much juice for any man.

As she turned around, looking for the toilet paper, she was awestruck at his master bath. She mouthed the word unbelievable while she pulled a stream of toilet paper from the roll and wrapped it around her hand several times, enough to wipe six behinds. She pulled her dress up around her waist, squatted, and wiped her soaked crotch. After tossing the used tissue into the toilet, she plucked away small pieces of tissue left behind from her wiping with her fingers. Then, she flushed the toilet.

Peering at her reflection once more, she adjusted her clothing, fluffed her hair, and pouted her lips. Her mind had shifted into fuck mode by the time she grabbed the doorknob. As she turned to leave, she spotted a bidet. She stopped and peered at the funny looking toilet.

What in the hell is that?

Moving toward it, she jiggled the handle and an up spout of water startled her as she quickly jumped back a few steps. Amazed, she tilted her head. Badly, she wanted to yell, "What is this thing?" but she decided against it, figuring this would not be her last visit. Besides she did not want him to know that she was not the worldly woman she was sure he was used to dating.

Gathering herself, she opened the door only to spot Reggie sitting topless on the bed.

Damn! What a remarkable sight.

Without uttering a word, she approached him and raised her dress above her thighs, up around her waist, and over her head. It left her fingertips and billowed to the floor.

He admired her beauty as his member fought to break through its denim restraint.

Kneeling before him, she rested her chin on his knee and unzipped his pants. Without warning, he took her by the arms and pulled her up to him. Their eyes met.

"Not like this," he said.

For a moment, she felt rejected and became crestfallen.

He smiled and said, "Oh, I do want you, baby," as if reading her thoughts. He admired her firm breasts and flawless complexion. "Oh yeah, I want you."

Maya stood up. "I'm sorry." She was completely embarrassed. The hooker in her came out at warp speed and she knew she had fucked up. She was too disgusted with herself.

No man like him is going to want a slut as his woman, she thought, with closed eyes, holding back the tears trying to push through.

She felt like crying bucket of tears. "I...I don't know what I was thinking. I guess...I don't know, it's been so long since a man has–"

He pressed his index finger against her lips, quieting her. "That's not what I meant, sweetheart."

Confusion replaced her saddened expression and her eyes widened with uncertainty.

Reggie proceeded to stand up and wrap his arms around her. First, it was tight, then a gentle embrace. He also buried his face in her neck.

Returning the embrace, she stroked her fingernails up and down his back. "I'm sorry," she whispered into his ear.

His voice was assuring to her. "Hush now, baby, there's no need to apologize. I'm the one who should apologize."

She pulled back, looked up, and gazed into his hazel brown eyes. It was too dark in the club to have noticed his beautiful, piercing eyes. "Apologize for what?"

"For not doing this as soon as you walked in the door," he said, his fingers pushing between her thighs, focusing on the swelling behind her full lips. Her juice oozed down his fingers.

Her taut thighs gave way to him and her body stiffened. She exhaled a soft gasp and tossed her head back, desperately holding on to him. He vigorously stroked her bud until it became engorged by his touch. Then for a moment, he nestled his finger inside the heat behind the thickness of her voluptuous lips. The palm of his hand took over where his fingers left off, massaging her fleshy knot. He pushed his middle finger farther until it curved inside her, searching the roof of her cave for her G-spot.

His discovery of the tiny bump ignited a blaze of passion as her hips gyrated against his hand. A surge of ecstasy rushed throughout her body as the tiny hairs stood on the nape of her neck. She felt like she had to pee again. She panicked. Her body tensed.

Swiftly, he turned her toward the bed and laid her down, his finger refusing to break its connection with her tiny bump. Her moans grew loud and deep and her body trembled. Her legs sprung up in the air and her toes pointed out like a ballerina. Instinctively, Reggie knelt before Maya and, without warning, he fervently sucked her swelling, stretching, and pulling it to its full potential.

In any moment, Maya thought her head would explode. She groped for the thick down comforter, balling it in her clutch.

"Ooooh, Lord, have mercy, yes!" she exclaimed, followed by repeated screams of ecstasy mixed with his name.

The sensation building inside her was suffocating. Her body quaked to his masterful work of cunnilingus, euphoria taking over and her cream squirting in his face. It took her several minutes to collect herself, but she rose to her elbows and gazed down at him between her thighs.

He smiled, licking his lips and savoring her flavor.

She sighed heavily. "Do you *always* greet your guests this way?"

He smiled and stood. She watched him from behind as he walked inside the walk-in closet. He was the most beautiful man, masculine and black from the top of his head to the tips of his strong feet. A sight to behold, ass so tight one could bounce a quarter off it.

Shaking her head, still feeling the sensation of the well overdue orgasm, she flopped back down on the bed, stretched her arms above her head, and closed her eyes.

Inside the closet, he removed his slacks, hung them neatly on the wooden pant hanger and slipped into satin pajama bottoms. He looked over his shoulder toward the bed and smiled. Had he found her? There was such an intense connection at the club the night before. Something about her that he could not put his finger on drew him into her. She was the honey and he was the bee, buzzing like a teen-aged boy following his first high school crush. He pulled a man's silk robe off the corner hook and headed toward her.

"How are you feeling?" he asked, tossing the robe over her face.

She pulled the robe down over her abdomen, sat up on the bed, and smiled. "May I have some more, sir?" she asked in her best *Oliver Twist* impersonation.

Amusement flickered in the eyes that met hers. "Only if I can wake up to that pretty face in the morning."

The full moon lit up the dark sky, stars looking down on Maya sipping Bailey's on the rocks. She was nuzzled in his armpit, her legs draped over his thighs.

He kissed the top of her head. "Are you chilly?"

Exhaling, she gently moved about, enjoying the warmth of his embrace. "No, I'm perfect."

Sipping Ciroc and Lemonade, he gazed off into the distance, admiring the manmade lake surrounding his palatial property. "So, Maya, tell me something."

"What would you like to know?"

"Whatever your heart desires."

Oh, he's good. "Well, let me see. I have three sisters and I live in Atlanta."

"And where are you amongst the four girls?"

"The spoiled-rotten baby," she chuckled.

He released a hearty laughter. "I bet you are!" He sat his drink on a small wooden table next to the wicker chaise they occupied and wrapped his free arm tightly around her. "What do you do for a living, Maya?"

Damn! Now was not the time to tell Reggie the truth. So, she crossed her fingers and lied. "I work for my sister."

"Really? Doing what?"

She made sure to respond quickly. "I manage her floral boutique." She had learned from Jonah that when you answer slowly, it meant you were lying and telling lies lead to harsh punishments.

And Maya will never forget Jonah's punishments that sent her back to Atlanta. How could one person be so damn mean? Because he was the pimp and she had become the Queen Bee of his stable. His top moneymaker and head bitch over all the bitches. Five years ago, Maya left Atlanta with a satchel and her thumb, hitchhiking three thousand miles to Los Angeles, determined to fulfill a lifelong dream. She was going to be a movie star. With not a dime to her name and no place to live, she copped a squat in front of Groman's Chinese Theater, but woke up in the city jail. Upon her release, she stumbled up and down Hollywood Boulevard until she bumped into the devil's spawn in disguise.

Jonah. Able to smell fresh tail a mile away, he fed and clothed Maya, giving her a place to live, camouflaging himself until the time was right. Once Jonah had Maya in his clutches, showering her with promises of love and everything her heart desired, it was time for repayment. The cost? Several johns a night, continuous beat downs and countless trips to the free clinic. However, one fateful night, Maya chose an audition over one of her regulars, and Jonah whipped that ass into submission, leaving her lying senseless and helpless on the floor of her apartment for several days without food or water. She thought she was going to die, being left to release bodily fluids and defecate on herself. Deep down inside, she found the will to live and made countless attempts to answer a ringing telephone. The last attempt was successful. Free came to her rescue by calling 911.

After spending days in the hospital, Maya returned to her apartment with a made up mind. She was getting out of the game. However, Jonah had other plans. Yet, little did he know, Maya's plans would succeed his when he took his last breath with a broomstick rammed down his throat and his body tossed down the trash shoot of her apartment building. The following day, Maya woke up in Atlanta, safe and secure.

After calling her name several times, Reggie waved his hand in front of her face. "Are you still with me, sweetheart?"

"Yes," she whispered, feeling a slight shiver from remembering the worst experience of her life.

"Where were you, darling?"

"Huh?" She still looked daze. "I'm sorry." She looked at her wristwatch. "You know, I really need to call my sisters to let them know that I won't be coming home tonight," she smiled.

Strangely, he looked at her and directed her to the kitchen, toward the wall phone.

"Thanks. I'll be right back." As she was about to walk away, she looked over her shoulder. "Would you like for me to refresh your drink?"

He extended his glass. "If you wouldn't mind."

She took his glass and headed for the kitchen. Placing the glass on the countertop, she closed her eyes and exhaled. Beads of perspiration danced about her forehead. She felt hot, like she was standing in the middle of the Sahara Desert. Her pulse quickened. Hyperventilation was on its way, but she was not having it. She was not going to give in to her fears. Jonah was dead and he could no longer hurt her. She caressed her forehead and closed her eyes. She inhaled deeply and exhaled. What was she going to do? She could not tell him that in a past life, which was exactly three months ago, she was the Queen Whore for one of Los Angeles' top pimps. A pimp she murdered, which means she was wanted for murder. But then again, the police had no idea who killed Jonah nor did they care. It was one less pimp on the street. So, for all she knew, she was safe. However, she had never met anyone of Reggie's caliber, who lived his lifestyle. The lifestyle she so envied Jade for living. Reggie could be her Jon Meadows and she could not risk messing it up.

Get yourself together, girl.

She looked around the kitchen and saw the phone propped on the wall. She took the handset from the cradle and dialed China's number. She patiently waited until the fourth ring before China answered the phone. "Yes, hello?" China's voice was groggy, awaken from a deep sleep.

"Hey, it's me."

China pulled up on her elbow and looked at the clock: 3:36 AM. "Hey, me, where are you?"

"I'm still at Reggie's."

"Okay, so I take it you're staying the night?"

"Yeah, that's why I'm calling. I didn't want y'all to worry. You know how Free can be."

"Yeah, I know. So, I'll see you in the morning?"

"Okay, but hey, China?"

"Yeah?"

"I need some advice."

China had to sit up in the bed for this one. "You're asking me for advice?"

"Yes, I know. It does sound strange," she chuckled. "But I really could use my big sister right about now." Maya's voice lacked its typical sarcasm, which brought on concern.

"What's wrong? Did that bastard do something to you? I'll kill–"

"No. No. No. Calm down, China. I'm fine. Actually, he's perfect."

"So what's the matter?"

"Reggie asked me what I did for a living and I lied."

"Oh… Yes, I can see your dilemma. Well, what did you tell him?"

"I told him that I managed Free's boutique."

China erupted in laughter.

"It's not funny, China!"

"I know. I'm sorry." She sighed heavily. "Do you want my honest opinion?"

"Yes, I do."

"Tell him the truth. Give him the opportunity to make the decision for himself. Now, I'm not saying you have to tell him every gory detail, but be honest with the man, Maya. Had Ron been honest with himself and me, Ashley and Andre would still have their father, and I would still have my husband. Being dishonest will get you nowhere, baby sis. Okay?"

"I'm scared..."

"Of what?"

"Of losing a good man."

"Maya, you can't lose something you don't have."

"Well, not yet anyway."

"Listen, be honest with him. If you *really* like him, then don't start out lying. You'll go crazy trying to remember every lie."

"You're right. I'll tell him."

"Good. But, like I said, you don't have to tell him everything. Tell him how your aspirations of becoming an actor led you to Los Angeles, and how you got involved with Jonah. You were in a strange place, you didn't know anyone, and the son of a bitch befriended you. Just don't tell him you fucked all of Los Angeles."

"Whatever, China, I'm trying to do right, damn!"

"Okay, I'm sorry," she lightly chuckled. "Listen, tell him that you had a bad lapse in judgment, your sisters came to your rescue, and now you're living in Atlanta with your sister, trying to get your life together."

Maya sighed deeply. "Alright, well I suppose I don't have anything to lose."

"No, but you do have a lot to gain. Trust me, sweetie, a man thrives on honesty. So, go have fun and I'll see you in the morning."

"Okay, thank you, China."

"You're welcome, and how's my car?"

"It's fine. Thanks for letting me use it."

"Uh huh, okay. Be safe and I love you—" China caught herself. She could not believe the words that came out of her mouth. But why not? She did love her sister. She loved all of her sisters. But, this was the first time she recalled telling Maya she loved her. And, it did not feel so strange either.

Maya extended the phone out in front of her. She could not believe her ears. Was she hearing right? China *never* uttered those three words to her before.

Slowly bringing the phone to her ear, she whispered, "I love you, too," before hanging up the phone.

That didn't feel strange because I do love my sister, even though she can be a true bitch.

Before returning to the deck, she refreshed Reggie's drink and admired the beautiful kitchen. She had never been in such an immaculate space before. There were more cabinets than she could count, and the floor was gorgeous—a deep burnt orange hue marble with light streaks of yellows that matched the backsplash over the countertop. Forty-two-inch cabinets the color of a summer sandstorm astounded her. If she were the woman of the house, the kitchen would definitely be her favorite room. She could definitely see herself as the woman of the house.

She returned to the deck and handed Reggie his refreshed drink before resuming her position under his arm.

"Is everything okay with your sisters?"

"Yes, everything's fine." She kissed him on the cheek. "I don't manage my sister's floral boutique."

"No?"

"No."

He listened intently.

She said a silent prayer and continued. "About five years ago, I hitchhiked to Los Angeles because I wanted to be an actor." She sipped her drink and then tapped the rim of the glass with her fingernail. "I wasn't fooling anyone but myself. I hadn't had acting lesson the first, but I knew I had what it took, so I though. But, what I didn't know was how hard it would be. Anyway, to make a long story short, when I arrived in LA, I was arrested my first night for sleeping outside of Groman's Chinese Theater..." She paused, waiting for a response from Reggie. However, he remained quiet. He listened intently. The lines that had formed across his forehead told her so.

She continued. "When I was released the next day, I was hungry, had no money and no place to go. I was too ashamed to call home. So, I met this man who offered to take me in. Me and my naive ass, I followed him like a lost puppy and ended up turning tricks." She held her breath and looked up at him to see the expression on his face. Nothing. Quiet as a mouse. "After a horrible experience where I nearly lost my life, my sister sent me a one-way ticket to Atlanta and now, once again, I'm just trying to find my way." She sipped her drink again. "I'm sorry for lying to you. I just didn't know what else to do. I mean..." She shook her head. "I don't know what I mean."

He sat his glass on the table and squeezed her tightly. Since they were having a coming to Jesus meeting, he felt the need for confession as well.

"Pretty girl, let me tell you a story. All of this you see—the house, the cars, the money..."

"Yes."

"Let's just say that you're not the only one with a less than appealing past."

Oh shit! Her heart started to flutter. *Not a damn drug dealer!*

"What do you mean?" she asked.

"I mean, I was able to get all of this by hustling drugs."

She pulled away from his embrace. "What? You told me you were an attorney."

"I am." He looked down at her and kissed her on the forehead. "Let me finish since we're coming clean."

He pulled her back into his embrace and she settled in to listen intently.

"When I was fourteen years old, I started selling drugs. My mom was a single parent; we struggled and could barely eat. I wanted to help my mom. So, I learned the business, and I learned early on to treat it like a business. I never partook of the products. I sold coke, crack, and pain killers until I was eighteen."

"Wow… You've been to jail?"

"No."

"Now how did you avoid not going to jail?"

"I was private with my business. I wasn't standing on street corners selling. That's where a lot of hustlers make their mistakes. No, I always sold after school, before my mom came home from work, and on weekends while she was working her second job. I called it the Candy Store. I also wasn't a dumb drug dealer either. I read books on business, and one of the things I learned was to take your money and make it work for you. So, instead of putting it in the bank, I invested my money in other businesses. And, by doing so, I was able to put myself through law school. Now, I own a couple of franchises and I defend drug offenders. How ironic is that?"

"Very…" she said, trailing off. His story reminded her of the movie *Sugar Hill*. He was her Wesley Snipes and she was his Theresa Randle.

"So, now that we've come clean, and neither of us have dirty hands, do you still want to get to know me because I surely want to get to know you?"

"Absolutely," she smiled, feeling relieved. She had met her knight in shining armor with flaws and all.

He smiled and kissed her passionately on the lips, his hand resting on her thigh. With each flicker of their tongues, his hand inched up her thigh, under his robe she wore, locating her soft, cushiony mound. Like an automatic door, her legs divided upon his approach. He parted her opening and raised her shell, exposing the pearl he would continuously stroke her until her body quaked several times with pleasure and, finally, exhaustion.

When she couldn't take any more, he kissed her on the forehead. "Get some sleep, pretty girl."

The next morning, Maya burst through the front door like a ray of sunshine, glowing. Barefoot, she dropped her shoes in the corner of the foyer and walked toward the sound of cackling hens in the kitchen.

"Good morning, bitches!" she said in a singsong fashion.

"Morning, slut," chimed China. "So, sit down and tell us everything."

"Yes, don't leave out one detail," insisted Jade.

Free remained quiet, anxiously waiting to hear about Maya's escapade with a stranger.

Maya grabbed a coffee mug from the cabinet and poured a cup of coffee. Pulling up a chair, she sat at the table. All eyes were on her. She smiled widely.

China was the first to ask. "Does he have a big dick?"

"China!" Free was appalled.

"What? Don't act like you don't want to know. Shit, I'm not getting any younger. I might as well live vicariously through her."

After sipping her coffee, she sat the mug on the table. She flashed a childish grin. "Yes, girl. It is big! I thought he was going to split me wide open!"

"Okay, do you have to be so doggone descriptive?"

"Oh, Free, hush," Jade said, smiling at her.

"So, did you tell him the truth?" asked China.

"Truth about what?" asked Jade.

"Yes, I told Reggie about LA and Jonah."

"Now why would you go and do something so stupid, Maya?"

"Because, Free, I wanted to start off on the right foot. I'm sick and tired of being a fuck up. Y'all tease me all the time about being a slut…" she paused and looked at China. "Especially you, China. Well, I'd rather not be associated with that label anymore, if you don't mind, you Black Widow."

"Fine. I won't call you a slut anymore. Now, tell us more."

"Well, you were right, China. Honesty is the best policy. Come to find out, I wasn't the only one with a past."

"Ut oh. He's been to jail, right?" asked Jade.

"Not once. He was too smart to get caught."

After Maya told the story of Reggie's life, she declared that she would definitely be back to Orlando. Soon.

CHAPTER 12

Atlanta, Georgia, Three Months Later

The sweetness of her nectar lingered on his tongue. Kneeling beside the bed, Samuel admired the elegance of his woman. Worshipping every inch of his jewel – her cute button nose, those adorable pouting lips and a deep, rich mocha complexion—he was filled with an aching love for Free. He battled the urge to roll his finger over her curvaceous figure lying beneath the satin sheet. Her fine hips and shapely thighs had ignited a burning fire deep within him. Images of the night before played pleasurably in his mind; visions of heated foreplay, explosive passion, deep moaning, and groaning.

He was convinced she was all he needed, and he was sure the feeling was mutual. With his eyes affixed on her beauty, Sam slowly reached down and retrieved one dozen freshly cut red roses he hid beneath the bed prior to the onset of their intimate evening.

Closing his eyes, Samuel silently whispered, "I love you more than you will ever know," before placing the heavenly scented bouquet on the pillow next to her delicate sleeping face and throaty snores.

Like a sponge, he wanted to soak up everything about his lovely Free. This was a special occasion and it was only befitting for his queen to wake up smelling roses. But he needed something else, which spoke forever to his lady in loud volumes. Reaching beneath the bed once more and retrieving a small Tiffany blue velvet box, he placed it on the pillow beside the bouquet of roses.

The next few moments felt like passing hours before she inhaled and sighed deeply, stirring about. When Free inhaled for the second time, the fresh rose scent aroused and awakened her from a beautiful sleep. She slowly opened her eyes to the man who had made the last six years intimately pleasurable, pleasingly intoxicating, and the single most loving experience of her life.

She smiled widely and unfurled her legs.

"Good morning," she said, followed by the stretching around of her voluptuous limbs beneath the covers, loosening muscles that had stiffened from sleeping in her favorite position—spooned by the man who astounded her with his presence. Although the curtains were drawn, her eyes were blinded by the brightness of the morning rays.

Her freshly woven braids were here, there, and everywhere. Sam plucked them away from her face with his index finger.

She stretched her arms above her head and stabbed her arm on a single rose thorn.

"Owww!" she softly cried out, grabbing her forearm and gently rubbing away the sting of the minor prick. She rose up on her elbows, adjusted her eyes, pulled her braids around to the back of her neck, and stared down at the roses and tiny box strategically placed on her pillow.

"What's this, honey?"

"Good morning, my queen," he replied, ignoring her question. "I trust you slept well. You snored like you wouldn't believe," he chuckled.

"Hush, I don't snore." She hesitated, pondering his comment. "Did I really snore?"

Sam raised his brow, smirked, and nodded his head before breaking into laughter. He had the prettiest row of teeth she had ever seen.

The faint smell of his cologne danced around her nostrils. She gently inhaled, drinking in his scent.

Then, embarrassment blushed across her face. "Loudly?"

Sam nodded and smiled once again, but this time a smile of contentment that he had made the right decision.

"Why didn't you wake me?"

"Are you kidding me? I needed the rest."

"And," she said, pulling herself up in the bed and leaning back against the high fabric-covered headboard, folding her arms across her chest. "What is *that* supposed to mean?"

"Never mind that now." He nodded toward the bevy of red on her pillow. "How do you like your roses?"

"They're beautiful and smell wonderful." Her frown instantly turned into a heart-breaking frown.

He leaned in and caressed her face. "Why the frown, babe?"

Her words were lodged in her throat and a burning sensation tickled her nose. Not wanting to cry anymore, the dam of her tear ducts were all dried up. Yet, one remained, which raced down her cheekbone, conjuring up disappointment as she shook her head. "I worked so hard...I can't believe I no longer have my shop."

His heart ached for her. "I know, babe, but don't worry about it. Soon you will have the money and you'll be able to open a new shop."

Her lips pursed tightly and she gave herself a soft tap against the head. "I was so damn stupid!"

"It was out of your control, Free."

"I had complete control. I was stupid for trusting her, but—"

"Baby, let's change the subject. I don't want you getting riled up this morning." He looked toward the gifts waiting for her attention. "Open the box."

She looked at the box.

Her mouth fell open as she realized what could be in it. "Samuel! Oh my God, honey!"

Sam took her hand in his and caressed it gently. "Sweetness, do you remember our very first date?"

Free's head lazily fell back against the headboard. Memories of the most embarrassing night of her life flooded her mind like an ocean's high wave crashing against the shores of Hawaii.

Why did he have to bring that up? she mused.

"How could I forget it," she chuckled bashfully. The thought of that embarrassing night still made her queasy. "I was never so humiliated in my life. I knew I should not have eaten so much crab, but *no*, I had to go against what I knew was wrong and shitted up and down the road. I still have nightmares about Port-O-Potties." She shook her head and released a hearty chuckle. "No, I'll *never* forget our first date, honey. Thanks for bringing it up." She playfully swatted at him.

Sam lowered his head and chuckled to himself. Despite Free's mishap with the public toilets, when he first heard the sound of her sweet voice, she had given him butterflies. After years of bachelorhood, Sam had given up on the notion of finding his soul mate. Actually, he was adamant one was nonexistent. That is, until he laid eyes on Free, a bevy of chocolate decadence.

Sam took her hand, held it close to his lips, and placed the most delicate of kisses on the tips of her fingers.

Chills shot through her as she fought to restrain the urge building between her luscious thighs.

"Baby, do you remember what I said to you on our first date?"

Now she was becoming antsy. What was with the fifty questions? If he was going to pop the question, she wished he would get to it. She was dying to open the tiny box. She knew it was a ring. It was the perfect size box.

"You said a lot of things, Sam." Her tone was annoyed and rushed; he recognized it quickly.

Sam reached for the tiny box and kissed her on the cheek.

Anxiety getting the best of her, she kicked her legs over the side of the bed, knocking the bouquet of roses to the floor, and darted to the bathroom.

"Woman!" Sam shouted, picking up the scattered stems and placing them back on the bed. "What are you doing?"

"I'm brushing my teeth," she yelled from behind the closed door.

"Couldn't that have waited?" A hint of irritation was in his voice. "Talk about ruining a special moment," he mumbled.

"It won't take long," she spoke with a mouth full of Crest.

Hearing her take in water, gargle, and spit into the sink, Samuel cringed. Seeing, let alone hearing, someone brush their teeth was the ultimate turn-off. He closed his ears to her teeth brushing and paced the floor, concentrating on how he would pop the question. *Free, will you please do me the honor of being my wife? Nope, that's too corny. Baby, you are the best thing that has ever happened to me. I don't know what I'd do without you. Oh geesh, Sam, you can do better than that. Girl, you are as fine as wine and I have to make you mine! Okay, now I am trippin'. Free, make me the happiest man on God's green earth. Free, I love you, babe, and…*

His thoughts were interrupted as Free exited the bathroom, gleefully skipping toward the bed.

Free picked up her roses and smelled them, before slipping her legs under the covers. She smiled widely at Sam like a child on Christmas morning.

Nervously sitting on the edge of the bed and pressing his palms against his thighs, Sam closed his eyes and said a prayer. He would not be able to stomach declining his proposal, even though deep down in his gut, he knew Free loved him. He never left anything to chance nor took anything for granted, especially his woman.

Free was getting antsier by the second. She snatched up the box and extended it toward him. "Here, hurry up before I change my mind," she said, smiling. She knew Sam all too well and he was not the best at this kind of thing. He needed a slight nudge, and nudged him she did. "Come on, man!"

Sam chuckled as he rubbed his baldhead. "So, is that a yes?"

"Yes to what?"

Sam laid his hand on Free's covered knee. "Woman, I love you. It's been six of the best years of my life, and I ain't gettin' any younger—"

"No long speech, just get to the point," she giggled.

"Nothing would make me happier—"

"Are you sure?"

A look of concern washed over his hazelnut complexion. "Do you have doubts?"

She took his face in the palms of her hand and whispered "None, whatsoever, my sweet, sweet baby," before tasting his lips.

"I love you, woman. More than you will ever know. I can't imagine…no, I don't want to imagine life without you."

The smile in her eyes contained joy and excitement for their future. "I know you do. I love you more."

Their lips met again. The softness of his lips pressed against hers made her hot in the tail. She could feel the internal rumbling of an orgasmic explosion coming on, taking her into an abyss of euphoric pleasure. She was ready to sex her man!

She wrapped her arms around his neck and held onto him, her eyes closed, deeply inhaling Unforgivable by Sean John she gave him for Christmas. She reclined onto the bed and cooed as their tongues frolicked.

His hands roamed over her shoulder, down her arm and across her breast, firmly cupping it with her breath caught in her throat.

Her breath was quick and heated, her chest heaving as he tugged and pinched her hardened nipple.

As their lips locked, his tongue formed a wet, warm sensuous trail from her bottom lip, down and around her neck, where he gently nibbled for a few moments. He descended down to her breastbone, under each breast where he took in her sweaty essence, continuing over her belly and down toward her love.

On cue, her legs separated like the Red Sea and allowed him passage. She caressed the top of his smoothly shaven head as she guided him toward the swelling protruding from the dark fleshy mound of her sweet heavenly love.

He parted her Brazilian-waxed full lips, exposing the tiny knot he planned to tickle, taste, and tease the bud he would enlarge as he gently stroked it. Fluttering and flickering, creatively capturing her clit, each stroke was as gentle as a feather and more intoxicatingly addicting than before.

She flinched when his tongue connected with her swollen rosebud. She stretched her arms above her head, plastering her palms flat against the headboard. The natural rhythm in her hips swiveled with intensity, building the desire she felt deep inside. It was a feeling she had never felt before…until she met Sam.

"Hssss. Ooooh, baby, that feels *so* good," she cooed, wrapping one leg around his neck. "Ohhhh, Daddy . . . ohhhh. . . yes, baby, yes!" she gasped for air as waves of pleasure consumed her, sending electric currents up and down her spine, connecting with the deep arch in her back. His concentration on the moist flesh drove her beyond crazy and into a whirlwind of euphoric, uncontainable pleasure. It was a feeling she yearned for each night; a feeling of having to urinate, but she knew it was much more than having to pee. That's just the only way she could describe it, but she knew that was the feeling of her juices building and building, wanting to break free and squirt all over his face.

Free's hips swiveled and gyrated wildly against his face, his tongue keeping full rhythm, not missing a minute of her beat. She crossed her legs at the ankles, her thighs snuggly caressing his head, rubbing with quick strokes against his mustache.

"Yes!" she yelled, grabbing the sheet and balling it into a fist. "Don't stop…baby. Right…there…damn it! Don't…you…stop…" As if struck by a jolt of lightning, her legs flew open and trembled uncontrollably.

Sam held on tight for the ride, his strong forearms holding steady to her gyrating thighs.

"Yes! Yes! *Yes! Ooooh, yes!*" It was extreme, like her head was about to disconnect from her body. "Okay, Sam, that's enough," she pleaded, wanting him to stop, thinking she simply could not take anymore.

It was overwhelming. Pure joy to the highest!

"Okay, baby!" she softly cried out.

She tried to push him away from her, but he was not having it. No, sir, he loved when she was in orgasmic overload.

Sam feasted on the sweet lava oozing from the opening of her steaming volcano until she broke into hysterical laughter.

"That tickles, Sam! Stop it!"

Finally, he stopped and gazed into her eyes, as he eased up in between her thighs and slid inside her slippery heaven.

Their tiny world of two meshing in the greatest of God's creations, together they danced as one.

Swirling seductively, submitting all of him, then retreating ever so gently, Samuel's deep strokes were as intense as the gaze they held.

Raising her legs and spreading them wide, Free released her hold on his hard shaft. He grunted as he slipped deeper into her abyss, his eyes still plastered on hers.

"For the rest of our lives," she panted.

"Until death do us part."

Free wrapped her arms around his neck and kissed him passionately. "Samuel?"

"Um huh."

"Are you sure you want to marry me?"

"I've never been surer of anything in my life. What about you?"

"I never block a blessing from God," she said as his body stiffened, expressing his seeds deep inside her.

CHAPTER 13

Free was out of control, pacing the kitchen floor, looking through drawers, opening and closing the refrigerator, and looking for nothing in particular like a rat on speed. She was getting married and she was ecstatic. Between her, Jade, China and Maya, she always figured she would be the one who would never marry, let alone find a man. For years, she had been mother hen to three younger sisters who provided enough turmoil to last her a lifetime. She loved her sisters, but she could not stand them one bit. Being in their presence had become a daunting task. If it were not for Sam, giving her the love and support she so desperately needed, she would have checked herself into a nut house a long time ago.

"Plans. I have to make plans," she said to herself, running about the kitchen, wringing her hands. "Oh, I don't know anything about planning a wedding," she said with a smile as wide as Ms. Celie's, and just as beautiful.

"What're you babbling about, Free?" Maya asked, entering the kitchen, making a beeline for the refrigerator. "What's for breakfast?"

"How about we go out for breakfast instead?" Free was unable to keep a straight face, moving about aimlessly.

Maya stared at Free wordlessly, her brows drawn together. "What in the hell is wrong with you? You're acting like somebody with no sense."

Free eyed the telephone mounted on the kitchen wall and a light bulb went off. "Quick, go upstairs to my room and wait until I tell you to pick up the phone."

"What? Why?"

"Just do it, Maya! Must you always ask so many questions?"

Maya stretched her arms high above her head and then scratched her backside. "This better be good," she huffed, jogging from the kitchen and up the stairs to Free's bedroom. "Okay, now what?" she yelled down the stairs from the top landing.

Free reached for the phone and dialed. "Give me a minute," she yelled. She listened for the dial tone.

Now in Free's bedroom, Maya sat down on the bed and patiently waited for Free's cue. She looked at the sheets and frowned up her nose at the dried stains. *They are so nasty,* she thought, yet smiling. She was happy for her sister. Besides, the more Free got laid, the less time she had to complain to her about anything and nothing under the sun, about something she was or was not doing. Free was definitely the mother she wished she never had, but since she was living under Free's roof, she had no choice but to listen to her daily bitchfest.

After the fourth ring, "Hello," came from the other end of the phone.

"China, hold on."

"Hey, honey. Okay, I'll hold."

"Free!" Maya impatiently yelled from the bedroom, such the brat.

"Wait a minute, Maya!" Free yelled. "I have to call Jade. I can't call with you on the phone."

Maya hissed. "Hurry up!"

Jade answered on the second ring. "Hey, sis!"

"Hey. How did you know it was me?"

"Caller ID tells on everybody," Jade chuckled.

"Okay, Maya, pick up the phone," Free yelled up the stairs and into the phone, causing Jade to pull the phone away from her ear.

Maya snatched the phone from the cradle. "It's about time. Why couldn't we have just used the damn speakerphone?"

Free chuckled. "Yeah, well, I guess I didn't think about that one."

"No, you didn't… What's going on, Jade?" Maya asked.

"Same shit, different day," Jade chuckled.

"Hold on, let me click China over," Free interjected. "China, are you there?"

"Yep, I'm here."

"China, hey chick. What's shaking?" Jade asked, delighted to be talking to her sisters. It had been a long minute since they had all been on one call.

"Damn, all of y'all on the line? Who died?" asked China. "Hey Jade. How are you? I haven't spoken with you in a while."

"I'm doing great and no one died. At least I don't think so. Have they?"

"How is Jon?" Maya asked Jade.

"None of your fast tail business," Free snapped, followed by a stifled giggle. "Always asking about somebody else's man."

Maya hissed and Jade responded with a slight chuckle. "Jon is doing just fine. He's away on business for a few days."

"How you like living in that mansion, Jade?" Maya asked. "You lucky bitch!"

"It's not a mansion, Maya, it's a loft."

"Stop hating, Maya," China interjected. "Free, what's up with the conference call?"

"That's what I wanna know. She's been running around here all giddy and shit," Maya proclaimed.

"Maya, I've told you I don't like that kind of talk in my house," Free reprimanded.

Maya sucked her teeth, which was typical coming from the baby of the clan.

"Free, what's going on?" Jade persisted.

Free hesitated before blurting, "I'm gettin' married!"

"What?" her sisters blurted in unison.

"You heard me. Sam asked me to marry him and I said yes."

China cleared her throat. "Are you sure that's a good idea?"

"Why isn't it?" Jade inquired.

"You sure he ain't no down low brother?" China asked with sarcasm.

"Naw, he's no down low brother. Not with all of the noise coming from Free's bedroom every damn night," Maya chuckled. "I never got that much dick when I was selling the ass."

"Maya, you find yourself a job yet or are you *still* free loading off Free?" China always knew how to put an end to Maya's diarrhea of the mouth.

"Fuck you, China!"

China laughed. "Typical. Grow a dick and I'll give up the pussy."

"Maya, what have I told you about your mouth?" Free scolded in a motherly fashion. "And China, I don't know why you talk so dirty either. You are a mother."

"What does my being a mother have to do with anything, Free? How about I can cuss because I am a grown ass woman? How about that, huh?"

Free sighed heavily. Not surprised by China's retort, Free took a seat at the kitchen table and played with packets of Equal, lining them up across the table.

"Alright, y'all, just once, let's not go there," Jade also scolded. "Free, I'm so happy for you. We all are happy for you, even though those of us don't know how to show it." Jade's sarcasm was directed toward China, and she felt it.

"Jade, keep your smart comments to yourself! I just want to make sure she knows what she's doing. That's all. When you think you know someone, you really don't. Besides, it hasn't even been long enough—"

"It's been long enough," Free said.

"Well he lives here, might as well get married," Maya blabbed.

China gasped. "Lives there?"

"No, he doesn't *live* here," Free said, beyond annoyed with Maya. She felt like smacking the taste from her mouth.

Jade sighed deeply. "Free knows what she's doing. Like you, China, she's a grown ass woman."

"I would hope so," China snapped.

Jade ignored China and asked Free, "Have you two set the date yet?"

"Yes, China, get over it," Maya quipped. "What happened to you won't happen to Free."

"I wasn't talking to you, Maya," China shot back.

"Damn, can we *please* have one conversation when there isn't any biting and snapping going on? One would think you all don't love each other. You act like enemies," Jade scolded. "And, quite frankly, I'm getting pretty damn sick and tired of this shit."

The phone line fell silent.

Free regretted making the call and broke the silence. "No, I haven't set the date yet, Jade. That's why I called. I don't know how to plan a wedding. I don't know the first thing to do. And I would like y'all to help me."

"We will help you," added China.

"Jade, will you be my maid of honor?" asked Free. Ooops! Talk about putting someone on the spot. She frowned up her face because she knew what was about to come next. She wished she had kept her mouth closed, but what was done was done. She could not take it back and she sensed the fireworks were about to erupt.

"Why was Jade selected to be your maid of honor?" China huffed.

"Aww damn, not this shit again, China."

"Go to hell, Maya!"

"Kiss my—"

"Shut up! Damn! Why must y'all always fuck up the mood? Why don't y'all just shoot each other and get it over with?" Jade yelled.

"China's husband already did that, what else you got?" Maya teased. She really did not have to go there, but it was in Maya's nature to pick at China any way she saw fit, which was constantly.

"You know what, Maya? I feel like ramming my foot so far up your ass, you'll feel my fucking toes tickling your throat, you trick ass bitch!"

"Enough!" Jade yelled. "Free, call me later and we will talk about the details. Yes, I would he honored to be your maid of honor."

"Well, I've got to run," China said solemnly, disappointed with hurt feelings, as she felt should be the maid of honor.

"China, please don't be mad at me," Free pleaded. "You can be my bridesmaid."

"I don't wanna be your damn bridesmaid."

"That wasn't very nice, China," said Jade.

"I have a great idea," Maya said. "Why don't we all be your honors?"

"Maya, you're a dumb ass," China barked. "That is some of the dumbest shit I've ever heard, you ignorant ass."

Maya remained quiet, but she was seething pissed. Only if China was in punching distance, she would channel Mike Tyson and TKO her ass. Pow! Right in the kisser.

Jade hummed. "Actually, Free, that's not such a bad idea. People have fifty bridesmaids. Why can't you have two maid of honors and one matron of honor?"

"Widow of honor is more like it," Maya quipped with pure, hateful sarcasm. She was on a roll.

This time, China ignored Maya for Free's sake. However, if Maya were in arms reach, she would surely wrap her slender fingers tightly around the tramp's neck until it snapped.

"That's not nice, Maya. You didn't have to go there," Free said. "I love the idea of having you all stand beside me and that's what we're going to do."

"Free, it's your wedding and I'll do whatever you want me to do," China agreed.

"Okay, it's settled then. I'll have three maid of honors. Let's touch base again next week. Okay y'all?"

"I can't wait!" Jade exclaimed. "I may be calling you before next week. The ideas are flying through my head already, girl."

"I don't want a big, fancy wedding, Jade. I'd like to keep it simple. Maybe something in the backyard…"

"That is so damn country." China fell out with laughter. "This is your first marriage and it shouldn't take place in your backyard, like some damn barbecue or family reunion. Come on, Free. You're not poor. You can afford to do more."

"It's not the money, China. You know I've never been one for being lavish."

"What's wrong with a church?" China retorted.

"Nothing is wrong with a church."

Jade interrupted. "Look, if Free wants to be married in an alley, then that's where it'll take place. Congratulations, sis!"

"Yeah, congratulations. Sam doesn't realize what he's getting," China said.

"What is that supposed to mean?" Free snapped.

"Will you stop being so sensitive? I'm saying Sam is a lucky man, damn!"

"That's not what she meant," Maya added. "If she could stop being so jealous–"

"Maya, I swear, you make my ass itch!" China shot back, ready to explode.

"You both make my ass itch," Jade snapped before turning her attention to Free. "Hey, Free. What about a honeymoon?"

"I haven't thought that far ahead."

"We need to have an engagement party, too," China announced.

Free thought of all the friends and family she does not have. "Who would I invite?" Her only family was the bickering cats on the phone.

"Friends, family, clients. . .a great way to bring in business, too," China said, but then thought twice. "Oh, wait. There are no more clients, thanks to Maya burning down your shop!"

"It wasn't my fault!"

"Yeah? Then whose fault is it, Maya? Who else was smoking crack in the back room? It sure as hell wasn't me. It wasn't Jade. And you know Free doesn't smoke that shit, you crack head. So, tell us who the fuck was it?"

A loud sob resonated over the phone as Maya was instantly overcome with emotions. "I do not smoke crack. I told you that I didn't know what happened, or how the fire started," she cried.

"Then what happened, Maya? How did you "not" burn down Free's business?"

"Okay, China. It's over with, let's just leave—"

"No! I won't leave it alone. We never really discussed it. How did it happen, Maya?"

There was silence.

In Manhattan, New York, Jade sat still on the sofa, her feet pressed firmly on the floor and breathing barely audible, waiting for Maya's response.

In Orlando, Florida, China grabbed her cup of coffee and strolled into the family room where she sat upon the burnt orange leather sofa. "Well, Maya?" she said, also waiting with bated breath.

"I really don't want to go through this again," said Free.

"Well, I do," declared China, "and I'm waiting on little sis to tell us she burned down your shop."

In Free's bedroom, Maya stood up from the bed and paced the floor. Pissed off at China's gall, she lay on the bed, the fragrant linens still smelled of Sam and Free's last lovemaking. She kicked off her shoes and rubbed her feet together. It was time to tell the truth.

"I was not smoking crack," Maya began, followed by a heavy sigh. "I was smoking a cigarette."

"A cigarette? Since when did you start smoking cigarettes?" said Jade.

"I've always smoked them. Anyway," she paused, gathering her thoughts being careful to use the right words. "Free?"

Still in the kitchen, Free walked over to the back door and peered out into the backyard. *The yard is large enough for a wedding*, she thought, not wanting to relive any of what was taking place over the phone.

"Free, are you there?"

"Yes, Maya, I'm here."

"I'm sorry."

"I know you are, Maya."

"So, you burned down Free's livelihood with one cigarette?"

"Yes, since you put it that way, but it wasn't intentional."

Jade cleared her throat. "I don't understand, Maya. What happened? Did you not put it out all the way, I mean…what? This makes no sense to me."

"Do you really want the truth?" Maya asked her sisters.

"You know what they say," said China, "the truth will set your ass free, honey."

"Alright." Maya turned over on her stomach, grabbed the pillow, and shoved it under chest. "It was slow that day and I was flipping through my *Essence* magazine. This dude walked into the shop and asked for a bouquet of lilies…"

"Let me guess," said China. "You put the cigarette down next to the Essence magazine and took old boy in the back of the shop and got your fuck on, right?"

Maya was silent.

"Oh, Maya, say it ain't so?" said Jade.

"Oh, it is so, Jade. That sounds like some shit she would do," barked China. "Free lost her business because you were hot in the ass!"

"I didn't fuck him," Maya mumbled under her breath. "I sucked his dick, alright. Damn, are you happy now? Free, I am so sorry. I didn't mean for any of this to happen. I burned your shop down because I'm a sex addict!"

"You're a whore. Plain and simple," China confirmed.

"That's enough, China," said Jade, shaking her head in disgust. *What in the world is this? Why must sisters be so nasty to one another?* "I don't know what the problem is with you and Maya, but you two need to get it together. You are sisters. When it comes down to the wire, you two are all each other have. I really think y'all should get some counseling."

"I agree, Jade," said Free. "Now can we please get back to my wedding?"

Jade sighed. "Wow, Free is getting married. You are finally happy and in love. I'm so excited for you, sis! I can't wait to tell Jon."

"Thank you, Jade. I'm excited for me, too," she giggled.

Then there was silence, followed by sniffling.

"Who is that?" Jade asked. "Is someone crying?"

The sniffling continued, followed by a deep swallowed.

"Is that you, China?" Free asked.

"Why does it have to be me?" China asked, blowing her nose into the phone.

"So you could be the center of attention," Maya teased. "Let Free have her moment. It's not always about you."

There was a gasping sound, followed by complete silence. Then a click.

"China?" Jade called out. There was no response. "Did she hang up?"

Annoyed, Free responded, "Yes she did and I can't blame her. Jade, I'll call you later." Free hung up the phone without saying good-bye and stormed upstairs to her bedroom.

While Maya sat on the side of the bed with the receiver held against her ear, Free marched in the room, making a beeline for her.

"I ain't done anything to China," she spoke into the phone to Jade. "She's always making herself—"

SLAP!

Free's open hand landed down the side of Maya's face, knocking the receiver to the floor.

"If China were here, I'd slap the shit out of her too!" Free yelled at the top of her lungs, clearly fed up.

Maya fell back onto the bed and grabbed her face. She was stunned. Her mouth opened and a floodgate of tears poured down her cheek.

"What in the hell is wrong with you?" Free yelled. "Why must you always act like you hate your goddamn sister?"

Maya sat straight up and with the quickness, snatched up the base of the phone and angrily threw it to the floor, and then jumped to her feet. "You didn't have to hit me, Free!"

"You're lucky I don't whip your ass!"

"You're lucky I don't whip your ass for slapping me!"

Free stood her ground and stared Maya down. "*Well*, little sister, if you *feel* you have what it takes to whip *my* ass, then by all means, work what you've got!"

From the receiver that was sprawled on the floor, Jade's screams echoed. "What is going on?"

Maya stood toe-to-toe with Free. A definite first. Never in her life had she felt the urge to do damage to her favorite sister.

"You feeling *froggish*, Free?" Maya took a step closer, their breasts barely touching. Face to face. "Leap and see what happens to your ass."

With bald fists and through clenched teeth, Free ordered, "Hang up my phone, get out of my room, and get out of my damn face before I leap on your ass alright!"

They stared each other down for a second, but it seemed like an hour. Neither would budge, fists in attack mode, waiting to retaliate with a powerful swing.

"Hello!" Jade yelled through the phone. "Free! Maya! What in the hell is going on?"

Maya took a step backward, slowly reached down, her eyes plastered on Free, and picked up the receiver. "Talk to you later, Jade, before she gets hurt," she softly said before placing the receiver in its cradle.

Free squared her shoulders, raised her chin, and balled her fist tighter. Standing tall and firm, if she was going to have to defend herself in her own house, she was going to go for the jugular. Then, she was going to put Maya out on her ass. She was not taking any shit from someone living under her roof, eating up her food, gawking at her man, and not paying any damn rent. What does love have to do with it? Not a damn thing!

Maya slowly circled Free like a big black raven circling road kill.

Free stood erect, keeping Maya in her peripheral vision. Now, she was not trusting Maya outside of her eyesight.

Maya stood in the doorway with her back to Free. Her head turned slightly, looking over her shoulder with a demonic appeal.

Free's chest heaved slowly, almost as if she were afraid to breathe.

"You make that the last time you put your fucking hands on me, *big* sister. Because I live in your house don't give you the right. I am a grown ass woman."

"Then act like it. Get a job and get your own goddamn place."

The bedroom door closed behind Maya, her stomping footsteps were loud and quick like a spoiled child throwing a temper tantrum.

Free relaxed her shoulders, released the breath she held, and sat on the edge of the bed. She lowered her head and closed her eyes. "This is supposed to be the happiest day of my life," she mumbled, followed by a stream of tears. "It's always something with her. I can't take this shit anymore," she whimpered.

She reached in the drawer of the nightstand and pulled out an aged photograph. She cupped her hands around the fragile picture, holding it as if it were a delicate flower.

She smiled and spoke to the photograph. "I wish you were here." The smile in her mother's eyes and the strong features of her father's face always made her feel better during trying times. Then it dawned on her. Who was going to give her away at her wedding?

She gently propped the photo against the base of the lamp positioned on the nightstand, curled up on her bed, and buried her face into the pillow where she quietly wept herself to sleep.

CHAPTER 14

The next morning, Maya sat at the kitchen table feeling anxious. She needed to get her own spot. Free had no right to treat her the way she did, just because it was her house.

That is some bullshit!

Getting her own place would be great, but exactly how was she going to do that without a job? She tapped her fingernails on the table. She needed to find something, even if it was Mickey D's.

Fuck that, I ain't flippin' no damn burgers. That's some high school shit. To hell with that.

She stood and headed toward backdoor. She opened it and inhaled Atlanta's early morning air. Her thoughts turned to Reggie. She wondered what he was doing. For the first time in her life, she missed someone. She actually harbored feelings for a man. For years, she was taught to turn off her feelings when it came to men. Getting the money was all she knew. Lay on her back, spread her legs, and two minutes later she was out the door with five hundred bucks.

The phone rang. It was Jade, asking what had happened between her and Free.

The last thing she wanted to do was rehash what had happened the previous night, but she responded, "Nothing. All is fine, Jade."

"You listen to me, girlie, and you listen to me good."

Maya leaned against the wall and folded her arms across her chest with the phone nuzzled in her neck. "Oh here we go with this shit again."

"Yes, here we go with the *shit* you are always bringing on yourself."

"Make it quick, Jade. I have things to do."

"You really need to get a grip on yourself. I don't know what your problem is or even what happened to you out in California..."

Her posture straightened. "Ain't shit happen to me in California!"

"But things must change. No, things *will* change. You are a grown ass woman, living off your sister who is about to be married, which means you have plans to make."

"Whatever, Jade. You are living off a rich ass man, so I suppose you can talk all that bullshit to—"

"I have a career, Maya, which is something you are seriously lacking. How about that?"

"Yeah, well, things will change. You do not have to worry about me. I plan to get my ducks in a row and move out, just as soon as I can. No worries."

"You need a serious attitude adjustment, too." There was a long silence. "Anyway, what happened between you and Free?"

"She slapped the shit out of me, that's what happened!"

Stifling a chuckle, Jade mumbled beneath her breath. "Good for you."

"I am sick and tired of my sisters thinking I'm some kind of child they can bully around."

"Oh, grow up, Maya! You are always whining and complaining about what someone has done to you. Do you ever stop to think that a lot of the shit that's being done to you, you brought on yourself?" Jade sighed heavily. "I love you, Maya, and I only want the best for you, but you have to take responsibility for your actions. Free's shop, for instance."

As much as she tried to remain selfish and stubborn, Jade's words, *I love You, Maya*, melted her heart. She rarely heard any of her sisters use those words and it felt good to know that Jade did love her despite her bitching and nagging.

"I love you, too, Jade, and I do hear you talking. I just," she sighed heavily, "get so tired of being treated like an outcast or something." Maya hesitated with a deep resounding sigh. "For once, when we are all together, whether it be on the phone or face to face, I want to be treated like a sister and not like someone who is hated or not wanted," she whined, which exudes naturally from her without recognizing it.

Jade hesitated before commenting. Maya was absolutely right and she was going to try her best not to treat her like a child, even though she acted like a fourth grader. "I will do my best not to make you feel like a child, but like my sister, because I love you with all of my heart."

"I love you, too, Jade," she smiled brightly, her heart a little lighter than before. However, she needed to clear the air with Free. Despite everything, she really did love her sister. "I have to go and talk with Free now."

"Okay, now, Maya, be adult about it. Don't be aggressive and argumentative. Besides, you know that's not Free's style anyway."

"I know, I know, and I won't."

"I still can't believe she smacked you."

"No, she smacked the *shit* out of me, that's what she did," Maya chuckled, not able to believe it either, still feeling the sting of Free's slap on the side of her face.

"Okay, call me back and let me know what happened. Okay?"

"Yep. Bye."

"Bye, Maya."

Hanging up the phone, Maya's keen hearing zeroed in on the footsteps above her head, which meant Free was out of bed. It was now or never. She needed to rectify things with her sister. She needed to make amends. She needed to ask for forgiveness.

Retrieving the carton of orange juice from the refrigerator, Maya grabbed a glass from the cupboard and sat down at the kitchen table. Silently, and in deep thought, she designed an apology as she sipped the extra-pulped juice.

Slowly descending the stairs, Free dreaded going into her own kitchen, and it bothered her. Before Maya moved in, her home held no animosity and it seemed like the only way she could rid her home, let alone her life, of her sister Maya, was to perform an exorcism.

When Free entered the kitchen, she made no acknowledgement and started brewing coffee.

Maya finished her orange juice, sat her glass in the middle of the table, and clasped her hands, threading her fingers. She closed her eyes and took a deep breath before she spoke.

"I think we need to put an end to this shit right now so we can get on with our lives. I'm going to start up a business so I can get out of your house."

Free sighed heavily, not in the mood to partake in Maya's game of mental manipulation. She remained quiet.

"You didn't have to put your hands on me either," Maya continued sarcastically.

Free tilted her head back and glared up at the ceiling, ignoring Maya, wanting to avoid a knock down, drag out fight, at all costs. *I need to paint before the wedding*, she thought.

Annoyed at being ignored, Maya reached inside the pocket of her fresh white cotton shirt, pulled out a cigarette, and pursed it between her lips.

At the striking of the match, Free whirled around in her seat and stopped her before she lit up. "What are you doing? You know I don't like smoking in my house."

"Trying to get a word out of you, so I did what I had to do."

"Not today, Maya, okay? I'm just not in the mood for whatever it is you're trying to dish out to me this morning."

Snatching the cigarette from between her lips, Maya lowered her head. "I'm sorry, okay? Are you satisfied?"

Free stood and propped her hand on her curvaceous hip. "No, I am not satisfied. What will satisfy me is you getting out of my goddamn house." She stormed out of the house and into the backyard where she would have solitude away from Maya.

Maya's mouth was like the opening of a tunnel: wide. She simply could not believe it. With her eyes on the closed door, Maya stood up and walked over to the window where she peered out at Free. Noticing Free's head tilted downward, Maya assessed that Free was crying and it was all her fault. A wave of emotions washed over her. Her heart felt heavy, tears welled in her eyes. Free, of all people, was the very last person she wanted to have as an enemy. Free was her rock. She was the only sister she *knew* she could count on and now their relationship was ruined.

What was she to do? With no job, no money, and no life, the road ahead was looking quite bleak for Maya.

The blaring ring of the telephone startled her. She gathered her composure, wiped the tears from her eyes, and reached for the screaming phone and answered it.

"Hello." While she tried to be as upbeat as possible, anyone who knew her could hear the pain in her voice, especially her man.

"Babe, what's wrong?"

The deep baritone voice engulfed her, bringing on a downpour of tears and snot. "Nothing," she cried.

"Why are you crying?" asked Reggie.

"Well," she reached for the roll of paper towels on the kitchen counter to wipe her face and nose, "Free slapped me–"

"She slapped you? Why?"

"Let me finish, Reggie."

"Okay, you have my full attention."

"It was my fault. See, Sam proposed to Free this morning and she was so excited. She called Jade and China on three-way and I was in her bedroom on the phone. One nasty word led to several nasty comments. You know how my sisters are, they treat me like I'm a child and they never have nice things to say to me and I…well, we all ruined Free's happiness…" she paused, taking a breath. "Free got tired of me and China going back and forth…

fuck this and fuck that...and well, she slapped me for being disrespectful in her house...and well...she told me to get out." Maya broke down in heavy sobs.

Reggie's heart went out to her. "Listen, babe, stop crying. You and your sister will be just fine. Maybe you two need your space. Why don't you come to Orlando for a little while."

"I can't intrude..."

"You're not intruding if I'm inviting you. Besides, that's why I called you. I miss you."

She perked up a bit. "You do?" She sniffed.

He smiled. "I do."

She could hear it in his voice. "Okay, when?"

"Is tomorrow good for you?"

"Tomorrow? Well, I guess...you're not giving me much time. I don't have any money."

"You have an open, first class ticket with USAir."

A smile graced her lips. "Okay. I miss you, too. I can't wait to see you."

"Then it's settled. I'll see you tomorrow."

"Okay, I can't wait."

"Bye, Maya."

"Bye, Reggie."

As she hung up the phone, Free walked in from outside. Their eyes met with apologetic stares. They stood in each other's space for minutes, but it seemed like hours before Free cleared her throat.

"Maya, I was wrong for slapping you." Free's voice reeked of defeat, waving the white flag of surrender. "I should not have put my hands on you, and for that I do apologize. But I meant everything else I said."

"I'm sorry, too. And you're right. I do need to stand on my own two feet. For years, you've been my saving grace and now I have to be an adult."

Free raised her brow and tilted her head to the side, unable to believe what she was hearing. Had Maya changed from thongs to the big girl panties?

"That's good to hear, Maya."

Maya walked over to Free and embraced her. "I love you, sis," she whispered in Free's ear.

"I love you, too."

Maya broke their embrace and exposed a wide smile. "Guess what?"

"What?"

"I'm getting out of your hair for a while. Reggie called. He invited me to Orlando for a few days."

"How nice. When are you going?"

"Tomorrow!"

"Tomorrow? Well then, you better get yourself packed!" Free exclaimed, happy she and Sam would have the house to themselves.

CHAPTER 15

Orlando, Florida

Tucking her hand in her pocket, China retrieved the letter Ron had written before his successful attempt at suicide. She sat at the kitchen table and, for the hundredth time since his death, held it in her hands, forcing herself to read the piece of lined paper ripped from Andre's three-ring notebook from the top.

Dear China, I do love you–she stopped, held her breath, and read it again. *Dear China, I do love you. I'm not well. I realize that now. What I've put you and the kids through is unforgivable. Especially Ashley and Andre.* Simple lines across the page, slicing her open, clean, and fast like a cold scalpel. Bringing back memories of pain, she cannot seem to bury no matter how much she tried. *I love my children, China. I never wanted to hurt them. I'm sick and I need help. My fascination with men. . .well that had nothing to do with you.* Oh God, she was losing her breath. *I'm so sorry. Sorry for everything I've put you through. . .the pain, heartache and tears.* She gasped, as if reading it for the first time. *I'm so fucking sorry. You should be tested.* She put her hand to her forehead, hiding the tears that trailed down over her nose and onto the kitchen table. *I've been tested and I'm clean. But, that doesn't mean you shouldn't be tested. You should be tested.*

"Dear God, what did I ever do to deserve this?" Her tears splattered, smudging the black ink.

Ashley stood in the doorway of the kitchen and silently watched her mother grieve, as she witnessed so many times before. She lowered her head and kicked at the kitchen floor like kicking up dirt at the playground. She walked over to China and wrapped her arms around her neck.

China tightly grabbed hold of Ashley and cried into her daughter's warm and comforting embrace.

"It's okay, Mama. Please stop crying. It's okay."

China cried uncontrollably. Something she had not done since the call she received from Marion, her dead husband's lover. China broke their embrace and wiped her face with the back of her hand. She glanced over her shoulder at Ashley, catching her glaring at the letter. Quickly, she snatched it up, folding it into fours, and tucking it away in her pant pocket.

"Where's your brother?" she sniffled, wiping away the residue tracks of salty tears.

Cautiously, Ashley took three steps backward. "I don't know."

"Didn't you two walk home together?"

"No." Ashley's head hung low with an idea of what was about to come next.

Whipping around in the chair, China glared at Ashley, standing still as words lodged in her throat. A chill came over her. Fear. "Where is your brother?"

"He wouldn't come when I told him to, so I left him."

Now standing, China squared her shoulders. Pursing her lips, she spoke slow and firm. "You *left* him where?"

"At. . .s-s-school," Ashley stuttered.

Calmness taking over, China relaxed her shoulders and grabbed the pack of cigarettes from the kitchen table.

"Why would you do that, Ashley? You know damn well you are not supposed to leave your brother. Damn it!" China felt like smacking her silly, but thought against it. She would probably do serious damage, considering how she was feeling, merely taking out months of anger and aggression on her daughter, and she wasn't too much in the mood for sitting behind bars with some big bitch named Bertha. She gathered her purse and keys from the foyer and darted toward the garage door. "Don't leave this house!" she yelled over her shoulder.

As China backed out of the driveway and into the street, Andre turned the corner. She sighed and pulled back into the garage. She stood at the top of the driveway and waited as Andre made his little hike up the hill.

"Hey, Ma!"

"Hey, yourself."

"You going somewhere?"

"Yeah," she nodded. "Looking for you."

"Well look no further, sexy mama, I'm right here."

China chuckled. "Sexy what? Boy, get your tail in the house."

"Ashley left me, Ma."

"Yes, I heard. She told you to come and you didn't move." She looked down at him with a stern face. "How many times have I told you that your sister is in charge when I'm not around?"

"I'm the man of the house now. I don't need her watching me. I'm supposed to be watching her."

China smiled inside. Her little man was trying to grow into a big man too fast. She knelt down before her son and playfully grabbed him by the arms. "When you can pay the mortgage, then we'll talk about you being in charge. And since that's not going to happen for at least twenty years, I'm in charge. Cool?"

Andre rolled his eyes. "Cool," he said, reluctantly.

Andre darted into the kitchen, drank a glass of milk over the sink, and peeled back a banana.

"What's up, little pussy?" Ashley teased, entering the kitchen.

"Kiss my ass, will you?" he shot back with seething venom.

"Mom!" Ashley yelled behind China as she headed toward her bedroom.

"Handle it on your own," China yelled back down the stairs. "You think you're grown anyway."

China retreated to her bedroom, closed the door behind her, and lay face down on the bed. The comforter still faintly smelled of Ron's cologne. She buried her face in the comforter, wrapping herself up in a cocoon.

You should be tested.

Ron's words haunted her. Being tested was something she had planned to do when she overheard his sneaky ass planning a rendezvous with his lover over the phone. Initially she was terrified. Suppose he had given her HIV? Suppose she was dying? What would happen to her children? She did not want to know. As long as she did not know, everything would be fine. Of course not. She was not fooling anyone but herself. She would be tested and she did. Three months ago and her test results were negative. Soon, she would have to take another test. This time, she would do the saliva test. The seventy-two hour wait damn near drove her insane. She could not put herself through that agony again.

Never in her twenty years of marriage would she have thought that her husband would desire another man. An affair she could deal with. However, having an affair with *a man* made her feel less of a woman. If it was anal sex he desired, she could have obliged. Well, on second thought, anal sex was not her type of thing. Anal sex, in her mind, was animalistic and she was not anyone's animal. Even though, she could be the biggest bitch in the state of Florida.

At a quarter to midnight, China peeled herself out of her cocoon and dragged herself to Andre's room. She opened his door to find him sitting, Indian style, on the bed watching television and eating a box of Hostess Ho Hos.

"Why are you up and eating that junk on a school night?"

Andre sucked his teeth and rolled his eyes. "Ma, you trippin'."

China's disposition became stern. "I beg your pardon?" Her head tilted to the side. This young man was truly getting besides himself. It had been three months since his daddy took his life and she recognized him wanting to be the man of the house, but she was still the mother and would always be two seconds from whipping ass, if needed.

"I mean," he quickly corrected himself, "It's Friday night. Ain't no school tomorrow."

"Pretend like it is and turn off that TV and open up a grammar book."

"Aww, Ma. I'm not sleepy. I want to watch *Creature Feature* anyway."

The lines in her face disappeared as the muscles in her jaw relaxed. "*Creature Feature?*" A gentle smile graced her lips. "I used to watch that when I was your age."

"TVLand has a Friday night horror movie since Halloween is next weekend."

China felt a little nostalgic. "Mind if I watch it with you?"

"On one condition."

China leaned back against the door and folded her arms across her chest. "Which is?"

"Can you make me a thick, vanilla shake?"

China stood erect and propped her hand on her hip. "Boy, don't you have enough junk in your round, pie face now?"

Andre slouched in defeat.

From the television, China heard the opening theme from *Creature Feature*. She darted toward the bed and climbed in next to Andre. "I'll make the shakes during commercial," she said, snatching up a Hostess Ho Ho and shoving it in her mouth. Since childhood, *Creature Feature* had always been one of her favorites. For an hour, she did not think about Ron or life.

CHAPTER 16

Manhattan, New York

Jon's mild-mannered personality is what Jade admired most. He took charge with quiet assurance and his determination to make her happy was always a priority. Even though he could afford anything in the world she could ever want, he gave her something more special, more real: love and security. She was secure in knowing her relationship with Joy was nothing short of a rest stop before reaching a more meaningful and stable one with Jon.

As Jade laid in bed, immersed under royal blue Egyptian one-thousand-thread-count sheets, she thought back to her first intimate encounter with Jon. That moment in Montego Bay turned her life upside down, inside out, and never to be the same again. Remembering his first kiss, sewn to her body, stitched into her skin caused a sensuous throb between her full, maple syrup-colored thighs. When he leaned in and gently stroked her bottom lip with his tongue before cupping her face and covering her mouth with his, she thought she would simply explode. As if it were yesterday, she remembered him slipping his hand under her blouse to find his way to her perky breast. He pinched her ripe nipples between his fingers. She shivered at the vivid vision.

"Ooooh," she released a soft coo, easing her fingers between her thighs, playing in her wetness and teasing the swelling taking place between the full mounds of her vaginal lips. With her free hand, she grabbed her breast and closed her eyes, wishing Jon's tongue would tease her instead.

Her ears perked when she heard the elevator doors to the loft open and a smile formed at the corners of her mouth. She flipped over on to her back and listened intently.

It was six in the morning and Jon was exhausted. His flight was delayed four hours, forcing him to take the last redeye from Los Angeles to New York. He loathed flying commercial, but he had no choice. His brother, Paul, had the jet grounded in Montego Bay. *Still fucking with the maids*, Jon thought of his brother as the elevator door opened to the four-thousand-five hundred-square-foot loft.

Stepping off the elevator, he sat his bags on the coal-colored marble floor, feeling relieved to be home. He closed his eyes and deeply inhaled Jade's scent. Christian Dior's Jadore wafted throughout the loft. He missed her badly and could not wait to hold her in his arms. Plus, he was extremely horny when he was away from her. His stomach still knotted with exciting anticipation of being with her.

Slipping out of his shoes, Jon untied his tie and rushed across the glossy marble floor toward the bedroom, abruptly stopping at the door, careful not to wake her. Tiptoeing into the bedroom, he loosened his tie before unbuttoning his pastel blue silk shirt. With nothing but moonlight peering through the floor-to-ceiling bay window, Jon peeped over at Jade. Anxious to slide in the bed behind her, he slipped out of the navy blue, pinstriped Versace suit and draped it around the wooden free form occupying a corner of the room.

With the ease of a cat burglar, he slid beneath the covers and pulled up close behind her, spooning and caressing. So close, the soft curly hair from his chest tickled her back. She softly giggled.

Planting a soft kiss on her ear, he whispered, "I've missed you."

"You have?" She smiled, so happy to have her man home. She had missed him more than he missed her.

Moving her beneath him, he planted kisses on her eyelids and down the bridge of her nose toward her lips. His tongue slipped inside the warmth of her mouth and played freely with hers.

Maneuvering her body into impossible contortions and positions to make his thrusts deeper until she screamed loudly with pleasure, Jon's momentum was swift, feeling every bumpy texture of her insides.

Her breasts bounced as she grabbed the calf muscle of her leg and pulled it back toward her shoulder, slightly bending her knee. Her moans and groans were deep and intense, and music to Jon's ears.

She gazed into his eyes as his deep strokes of love brushed against the tiny bump nestled at the roof of her love.

"Woo, baby, I love you so much," she cooed.

"I love you," he panted.

Feeling the anticipation of exploding inside her building rapidly, he slipped out of her and straddled her face.

Jade took hold of it, first roughly, desperate. Then, she held it lightly, delicately, like it was made of blown glass, a goblet from which she wished to drink. Bringing it toward her mouth, she began to speak into the head of his hardened flesh.

"I hate to waste good seeds," she said as she took him inside the warmth of her mouth.

The hotness of her breath, combined with the excitement he felt as he watched her cheeks sink in, rapidly increased the anticipated release rushing from his jewel sack to the tip of his head.

He yelled from deep within as his seeds swished around her lips and oozed down around her chin, dripping onto her chest. His final thrust and jerk against her mouth alerted her of the conclusion of his release.

"Welcome home," she smiled, looking up at him. As she watched him recover, she stroked the tip of his penis with her tongue.

He shivered. "Hey," he said, grinning. "That tickles."

She patted him on the behind. "Come on."

Jon dismounted her and rolled over onto his back. "I'm exhausted."

"I bet you are," she laughed, walking toward the bathroom.

Jon watched her shapely behind sway in unison with her long blonde twists hanging below her shoulders.

"How was your trip, babe?"

"Tiring, but productive."

"And less stressful without Paul, I'm sure," she chuckled.

Jon nodded at her comment. Paul was more of a distraction than an asset. However, he was his brother and Jon believed in a tight family bond.

After Jade brushed her teeth, she turned on the shower.

"I closed the deal," he said, contemplating showering with her. If only he could get his body to move with his thoughts. He was worn out.

She stood in the doorway, the silhouette of her body made him rise once again. "That's great, babe. So this means you'll be traveling to LA quite a bit, huh?"

Now sitting on the side of the bed, Jon stood to his feet and stretched his arms above his head. "Yeah," he yawned, "this is a three-year project."

"Well, if anyone can do it, you can!"

Jon walked toward the sound of her voice and stood in the doorway of the bathroom. "Yep, as long as I have your support." He smiled at her, his penis aiming directly at her cave.

Jade looked down and laughed. "Down, boy."

Jon opened the glass shower door. "I don't know where he's getting all of this energy because I'm whipped." He stepped into the shower and stood under the steaming hot four-headed waterfall.

Jade stepped inside, closed the door, and moved in close to him, pressing her chest against his.

He lathered his hands with soap, wrapped his arms around her, and washed her back.

She rested her head against his wet shoulder. "Guess who's getting married?"

"Who?"

"Free and Sam. She's so excited!"

"Yeah? That's great, babe."

Jade wrapped her arms around his waist and stroked his behind. "I'm going to help her plan it."

Jon tossed his head back and immersed his face under the stream of water and shook his head; his short-cropped curly tresses released water like a wet dog. "I'm sure it will be beautiful."

"First China, now Free, I wonder who will be next."

Jon smiled inside. He caught the hint, but said nothing and kissed her on the forehead before exiting the shower. "I'm beat. That was a long ass flight."

Still in the shower, Jade lathered down with Warm Spirit's Heavenly bath gel. "I could call in. That is if you don't have any meetings scheduled," she yelled out to Jon, before rinsing off.

"As a matter of fact, Veronica cancelled all of my appointments for today. She knows me well, I guess."

"Great, we can do lunch and–"

"What, no breakfast?"

Stepping out of the shower, she reached for the oversized terrycloth robe and wrapped herself in soft bliss. Hearing him loud and clear, she stood in the doorway of the bathroom and dropped the towel down around her wet, French manicured toes.

Lying on the bed, Jon rose up on his elbows and smiled ear to ear. "Now, that's what I'm talking about," he said, ready to feast on the delicacy between his woman's toned thighs.

Jade teased him with each slow step she took, her round apple bottom swaying in harmony with her firm tear-dropped shaped breasts.

As she reached the edge of the bed and Jon pulled back the covers, the intro to India.Aire's "Brown Skin" exuded through the radio on the bedside table. Just as India's sensual melodic words, "Brown skin," bounced off the walls, Jon's encore was deep inside of Jade, slowly and gently stroking to the deep heart-thumping of India's bass, their brown skins meshing, unable to tell where he began and she ended.

"Oooh, *yes*," she whispered into his ear. "Mmm, my, my, my… ahhh."

"Ohhhh," he deeply moaned, his lips planting delicate kisses behind her earlobe as he dipped in and out of her tightness.

"Jon, baby, you do me *so* good!"

Cupping her face, he looked into her eyes. He loved the way they would roll upward with each deep intense stroke he ensued.

"I love you, Jade," he lovingly declared as the head of his hardness stroked the top ridges of her cave, causing small shivers to shoot throughout her.

Her moans, deep, yet soft, were a sweet melody to his ears and the fuel to a never-ending flame that burned deep inside for her. She was his soul mate and the love of his life. He longed for her kisses, touches, and essence. And at that very moment, Maxwell crooned "Whenever, Wherever, Whatever." Jade completed him and he was more than confident she felt the same. They were like inseparable Siamese twins. Moreover, he did not want it any other way.

Major Harris's "Love Won't Let Me Wait" created the finale to their crescendo of orgasmic symphony.

A single tear pushed its way down her cheek. His love always made her cry tears of joy.

With her back to him, Jon spooned her, inhaling her natural intoxicants and sending him into yet another drunken haze of desire. However, he maintained control and would save some for later. Although his rising nature was misbehaving as it gently pressed against the firmness of her round bottom.

She smiled at her ability to induce urges within him without doing a thing. Knowing her man was constantly turned on by her thrilled Jade to no end. And she was confident that this was something that would never dissipate for he ignited those same urges throughout her as well.

"So, let's talk about LA," she said, stroking his arm.

Jon pulled her in closer, closing up any space between them. "What about LA?"

"You said something about buying a place there. Are you thinking about permanently relocating there?"

"This is a three-year project. I suspect we would need a place we could call home."

"We?" Jade echoed. A huge smile exploded across her face. She loved it when he included her in his plans. "Baby, what about my job?"

"You really don't have to work, you know? I have plenty of money. I can take care of you."

"I know you can, baby, and I do appreciate your saying that. However, I do not want a man *taking care of me*. I like being independent and having my own–"

"Alright, Destiny's Child," he chuckled.

She playfully smacked his hand and sung, "I've bought it…"

"But seriously," he softly said, "I do want to buy a place in the Hills."

"The Hills?"

"Beverly Hills. Nothing big though, but a nice place we can make our home when we travel between there and New York."

Beverly Hills. Rodeo Drive. Venice Beach. Shoot, I'm ready to quit my job now!

Excitement shot through Jade. Never in her wildest dreams did she think she would be wrapped like a fajita in the arms of a millionaire, let alone being in love with one.

She quickly retorted, excitement flowing at warp speed from every word she spoke. "I could probably find a job there. And I'm sure they would pay more, too."

"Well," Jon whispered, kissing the top ridge of her ear before stroking it with his tongue. "Here is what I'm thinking."

Chills shot throughout her. *Lord, Jesus, this man knows all of my hot spots and he's not playing fair!*

"I'll have Veronica find us a realtor," he continued, his hand caressing the outline of her curvaceous hip. "Schedule an appointment and you can fly out and look at homes. And whichever one you like, that's the one we'll go with."

"What? I can't make that kind of decision, Jon. I...I don't think I want to."

"Sure you can. Babe, I need you to do this for me. I'll be too busy on this end trying to work out the kinks in this deal and start the ball rolling. But if you don't want to, then I can have Veronica do it."

Her feminine instinct kicked in. Another woman picking out the home where she and her man were going to live? There was no chance in hell of that happening. Veronica was her girl, but she had learned her lesson once before and she was not a second go-round fool. When it came to her man, she took good care of him.

"No, I'll do it. I'll take vacation time and spend about a week in LA. That should do it, don't you think?"

"Yes. Now," he shushed her, softly pressing his finger against her pouting lips, "you call in and I'll get a quick cat nap in before it's time for my lunchtime feeding."

"Greedy ass," she chuckled.

He caressed her tightly, and as he kissed her locks, he deeply inhaled her favorite scent, Patchouli. "You're the biggest part of me."

"And you me."

CHAPTER 17

Atlanta, Georgia

Jade pleaded over the phone. "Go with me, please! I don't want to go by myself."

"I don't know, Jade. I have so much to do..." Free sighed heavily, shaking her head. "Maybe I can get away for a weekend."

"Yes, Sam can do without his woman for a couple of days."

"Shoot, why not?"

"Great! We can leave Friday night and return Sunday."

"Sounds like a plan to me. Just let me know the specifics and I'll get my plane ticket."

"Plane ticket?" Jade chuckled. "Chile, please, we are taking the jet!"

"Oh goodness," Free laughed. "Listen, I have something to tell you, but I don't know if I should say anything or not. You know I don't like to share or get into folks' business."

"What is it?"

Free sighed. "Nothing. On second thought–"

"Oh, no you don't," Jade interrupted her. "You're not getting off that easy. You have something you want to tell me, but you're not sure if you should tell me. Right?"

"Uh huh."

"So spill it," Jade said excitedly. "I haven't heard any good gossip in a long time."

"Humph, not sure I would label this gossip."

"What it is, Free?" The tone in Jade's voice shifted to concern.

"The night before Ron's funeral, China laid something really heavy on me and I've been trying to wrap my mind around it."

"Will you please tell me." Jade was growing impatient and it reflected in her voice.

"When Maya was sixteen, she and Ron..." she trailed off, cringing at the disgusting thought, unable to find the appropriate words.

"What? I'll kill his ass!" Jade snapped. "Fucking with my sister!"

"Watch your mouth and he's already dead."

"He's one lucky bastard!"

Free could hear Jade's teeth grinding, which was typical Jade when she was angry.

"Why are we just finding out about this now? We need to call China–"

"No," she blurted, "don't call China. She has enough to deal with and, besides, she said that Maya was a willing participant."

There was silence.

"My Lord," was all Jade could muster. "Everyone in this family needs counseling."

"Speak for yourself, honey. I am just fine."

"Really, Free. This is just unbelievable." Jade hissed. "I don't put anything past Maya and neither should you."

Free could hear Jade moving about in the huge loft she shared with Jon. Her footsteps echoed in Free's ear. "I don't have to worry about Maya. Sam wouldn't touch that tuna with a ten-foot-pole."

Jade fell out with uncontrollable laughter. Free rarely used profanity or spoke negatively against anyone. But when she did, it was hilarious to all who were in earshot.

As Jade continued her laugh fest, Free thought of California and grew more excited about the idea. She had not had a vacation in years and it would be nice to get away, especially with Jade. She was the closest to her than China or Maya. It would be nice for her to experience something new with Jade. "Okay, when are we leaving?" she blurted with excitement.

"Let's go next weekend and you know what? How about we shop for your wedding gown while we're there? With all those fancy designers, we are bound to find something you will like. Maybe Vera Wang…"

"Sounds expensive to me."

"Be cheap with the flowers, the cake, and the bridesmaid's dresses, but *don't* be cheap with your wedding dress, honey."

"Alright now, I can't wait! Listen, sis, I have to run. Call me back with the details. Love you!"

"Okay. I love you, too. Tell Sam hello for me. Bye."

"Sure will and a hug to Jon. Bye, bye."

Unable to contain herself, Free slammed the phone on the hook and released an excited sharp shrill that rushed a panicking Sam into the kitchen.

Out of breath he said, "What's wrong, babe?"

"You won't believe it. I'm so excited!"

"Try me."

"I'm going to *Cal-i-forn-i-a*!"

CHAPTER 18

The next morning, Maya strategically picked out the sexiest negligee, thongs, and panties she owned and tossed them into an oversized duffle bag. Her flight was leaving in less than four hours. Excitement washed over her, giving her a renewed sense of self and love. Hell, who was she kidding? Her ass was on fire and Reggie's hose was all she needed to douse it. The last few months with Reggie have been blissful, her traveling back and forth to Orlando on his dime. Early evening phone calls turned into late nights of passionate phone sex. Finally, a true relationship with a man who does not care about her flaws or her past work history. Reggie was the outlet she needed and she was taking full advantage of it, too.

Moving from her closet to the duffle bag, Maya neatly folded several pairs of jeans and cotton shirts, and strategically placed them in the bag with her toiletries. Never turning around, she sensed Free standing in the doorway. It was so like her not to knock, just open the door, and come right on in. After all, it was her house to do as she pleased.

With her back to Free, Maya acknowledged her presence. "Hey, sis, what's up?"

"Not much just wanted to tell you that I'm going to California with Jade."

Swiftly, Maya faced Free and asked, "Am I not invited?"

"Aren't you going to Orlando?"

"Yes, but–"

"But you have a great time and I'll see you when you get back."

"Fine," Maya huffed as she continued stuffing clothes into the duffle bag.

"It's not a big deal, Maya. Plus, I think it's great that you're going to Orlando." Free took a seat on Maya's bed and started sifting through her duffle bag.

"You do?"

She pulled out a lime green thong from the duffle bag and held it up. "Yes, I do and what is this?"

"A thong. Maya snatched the colored string from Free's grasp. "Go to Victoria's Secret and get you a couple. I'm sure Sam would love them."

"Child, please, I am not wearing a string in the crack of my tail. I'm sure they can't be very comfortable. Besides, if you're only going to wear something this skimpy, then why wear anything at all?"

Maya tossed the thong back into the duffle bag. "So your man can take it off."

"Just nasty," Free huffed.

CHAPTER 19

Orlando, Florida

Orlando International Airport swarmed with vacationers and Maya's bladder was about to burst. She eyed the sign that read WOMEN and rushed toward it, weaving through the ocean of travelers with her duffle bag flung over her shoulder.

Inside, a stench brought her to abrupt halt. She pinched her nose closed. "Good Lord," she whispered, trying not to take in any air through her mouth. *Smells like something crawled up in that ass and died*, she thought as she made a beeline for first stall in sight. She wanted in and out. The last thing she wanted was to meet her man smelling someone else's shit.

She dropped her duffle bag to the floor, resting her purse on top of it. She glanced at a paperback copy of *Anything Goes* by Jessica Tilles protruding from the side pocket of her duffle back, thinking she needed to finish the book on the plane ride back to Atlanta. It was the Book of the Month for G.A.A.L. Book Club of Atlanta, a club she joined last month because she was bored out of her mind and needed adult interaction with someone else other than Free and Sam.

With her bladder on full, she did a little jig as she fumbled with the zipper on her jeans, quickly pulling them down around her ankles. She squatted, steadying her weight on her legs, being careful not to move. Her muscles relaxed and she slowly exhaled as urine exited her bladder, making its way through the urethra, splashing into the awaiting water in the toilet bowl.

Ooops!
She slightly moved.
Shit! Shit! Shit!

Urine splashed on the toilet seat and down her thighs, trailing to her jeans and dampening them. Disgusted, she pulled a long stream of toilet paper from the dispenser attached to the stall and wrapped it around her hand several times before wiping herself and disposing of it into the toilet. She grabbed another yard of toilet paper and blotted it against her jeans.

Damn it!

She was too through. The last thing she wanted was to meet her man with a huge piss stain on her pants. Well, there was nothing she could do about it now, so she pulled up her pants. As she tossed her purse and duffle bag over her shoulder, her cell phone started to ring. Unlike other passengers, Maya never turned off her cell phone as instructed by the Southwest Airlines flight attendants.

Again, the duffle bag hit the floor. She opened her purse and dug deep into the bottomless pit and felt around for the cell phone. Grabbing it, she flipped open the phone. It was Reggie.

"Hey, baby!"

"Hey, you. I see you landed safely."

"Yes. You waiting for me in baggage?"

"No, baby, that's why I'm calling you. Had to handle some business. One of my clients got his ass locked up on a drug charge, so I need to hit the county jail."

"Oh?" Disappointment drenched her voice.

"I've sent a car for you. The chauffeur is waiting for you in Baggage Claim."

"How will he know who I am?"

"He'll be holding a sign with your name on it. Look for it."

"Will you be home when I get there?"

"I'll try my best, but I don't think so. Listen, the driver will give you the key. Make yourself at home and I'll see you later."

"Oh, okay then."

"Hey."

"Yeah."

"I can't wait to see you, beautiful."

She smiled. She felt like pinching herself, this all seemed unreal. "I can't wait to see you, too."

She closed the phone and jammed it back into the bottom of her purse.

She picked up the duffle bag and rushed out of the stall. She quickly washed her hands and rubbed them dry on her jeans before heading to Baggage Claim.

She wondered why people were taking their sweet time walking through the terminal as she began to get irritated. She felt like pushing them all to the side. She knew it was wishful thinking to ask God to part the flood of travelers like the Red Sea so she could get through. Anxiety mounted as she weaved around people with kids, people in wheelchairs, people holding hands and strolling as if it was a warm sunny day in the park. People, people, and more people!

"Excuse me!" she snapped, pushing her way through the crowd of people, trying to make her way through the never-ending terminal. When she saw the elevator, she felt like she would pee again from excitement. She was that much closer to seeing Reggie and getting out of that damn airport. Never mind the fact that she's terrified of flying anyway.

As the elevator descended to Baggage Claim, a tall white man dressed in a starched black suit and cap held a sign that read MAYA HOWARD. Quickly, she approached the man with a huge smile.

"That's me. I'm Maya Howard. I have to get my bags."

He nodded and followed on her heels as she hurried to Carousel 9. To her amazement, her bag was the first to hit the conveyor belt. It was going to be a good after all.

She pointed. "There it is."

The chauffeur grabbed her bag and they headed out of the airport and into the Florida sun. She loved Orlando. She could definitely see herself living there. With Reggie, of course.

When they arrived at the shiny black Lincoln Town Car, he opened the door for her and said, "Welcome to Orlando, Ms. Howard."

"Thank you," she said, smiling and thinking she could really get used to this kind of treatment. "Oh, Mr. Hamilton said you should have something for me."

"Yes, ma'am." He replied, reaching inside his pant pocket. He pulled out a key and placed it in her hand.

She folded the key into her grasp and smiled at him. She climbed inside the vehicle and settled in for the forty-five minute drive.

CHAPTER 20

Maya watched as the Town Car drove down the spiral stoned driveway, disappearing out of sight. She channeled her inner Mary Tyler Moore and spun around with her arms stretched out wide. The view was breathtaking. She made it a point to take it all in every time she visited Reggie.

Maya had not loved too many men. In fact, she truly had not loved at all. She had no clue about love, what it was, or even what it felt like. But what she did know was that Reggie made her feel special. Like teenagers, they talked for hours over the phone, talking about this, that, and the other. They talked in great lengths about their pasts and their expectations of the future.

Maya inserted her key in the door and pushed it open. She picked up her bags and carried them into the foyer, dropping them to the floor and closing the door behind her. She tossed the key on the small table tucked in the corner of the foyer. Attached to the table was a note. She leaned in closer and, without picking it up, she read it.

My Sweetness,

I've missed you. Come to me, baby. Follow the rose petals to your man.

Love,

R.

Maya looked toward the staircase. Her mouth flew open at the many red rose petals adorning each step. Hurriedly, she dashed up the steps to the master bedroom. Stopping suddenly, she grabbed hold of the gold door knob and took a deep breath. She did not know what to expect. She was nervous; butterflies fluttered in her stomach. Throwing all excitement to the wind, she opened the bedroom door and was immediately kissed by Natalie Cole's "I Can't Say No" and the vision of Reggie sprawled across the bed.

He remembered! She had told him that she loved Natalie Cole.

"Hey, baby," he said with a smile.

That smile. She absolutely adored that smile—white, bright, and connected to the most beautiful dimples she'd ever seen. That was her man and she was going to make his toes curl.

Smiling, she walked toward the bed, stripping out of her clothing one article at a time. By the time she reached the bed, she was wearing what he loved to see her in—absolutely nothing.

"You're a beautiful sight, Reggie," she said, stroking her bottom lip with her tongue.

"So are you," he added, really turned on by her charm.

"Hey, I thought you were dealing with a client?"

"I lied, so sue me," he teased. "Now, if you don't bring that ass to me, we're going to have a problem."

"Absolutely, Counselor," she said, straddling his legs and scooting backward, resting her round rump on his ankles. She grabbed the silk sheets in her clutches and leaned down, her eyes to his *one eye*. She puckered her lips and blew her warm breath on the tip of his manhood.

He shivered. Everything about Maya excited him. Before Maya, Reggie had no interest in marriage, let alone a relationship. Being tied down to one woman was not a preference as he adored many women—a different woman each night of the week. He enjoyed and held a special connection with each woman, even though it was understood that his intention was purely sexual and nothing more. However, all of that changed the night Maya Howard sashayed into Breeze's Night Club. She was beyond breathtaking and he thought his heart would stop when he saw her. Never had a woman had such an effect on him. Now, he could not get enough of her. He wanted to breathe and drink up Maya every single day. In order for that to happen, he needed to make an honest woman of her. However, it simply wasn't the time. Will there ever be the right time? Commitment scared the shit of him.

She loved teasing him. She loved watching his toes flinch. She loved the permanent smile his lips held when she pleased him. Like a lioness on the prowl, she crawled up his legs and hovered over her prey.

He grabbed her hips.

She moaned at the gentle touch of his strong hands.

He stared into her eyes, adding pressure to her hips, guiding her down on his hardness.

When he entered her, she tossed her head back and arched her back.

He deeply moaned and slowly moved his hips up and down.

Her hips met the rhythm of his creating a hot sexual melody, and it was on for the rest of the night.

CHAPTER 21

The next morning, Reggie cooked Maya breakfast. A natural Betty Crocker, he sung silly songs as he flipped pancakes and smeared them with homemade pear preserves, a treat he learned to make as a child while spending summers in Emporia, Virginia with his grandmother. Even though he's a guy's guy—with a strong back and muscular build—he's remarkably domestic. Like Maya, his mother was also killed in a car accident when he was sixteen, and his father was a rolling stone, so he had to fend for himself. He taught himself how to cook, do laundry, and even iron. He loved decorating, too. Every decorated space in his palatial home has his name written all over it.

"Hmm, something smells wonderful," Maya said, entering the kitchen wearing absolutely nothing.

Reggie peered at her and smiled with lust. He was tempted to bend her over the kitchen sink, but he didn't want breakfast to get cold. "I love that outfit," he said, followed by a hearty chuckle that always warmed her heart. Maya loved his laugh.

She said nothing. She raised her buttocks on the leather stool in front of the kitchen island. She was blissfully happy in the twenty-four hours before she saw him and while she saw him, then overwhelmingly sad when they were apart. She knew this wasn't healthy. She couldn't diet or exercise *this* toxin out of her bloodstream.

Maya fought the urge to tell Reggie that she loved him. She was too proud to be the first one to say it. No, that wasn't it. She was afraid that as soon as she told him, he would run like hell. To men, the words "I love you" meant "I want something from you," as though you wanted to harvest a kidney from them. Maya didn't want anything from Reggie. She didn't want anything, yet she wanted everything. She wanted to live the life that he could afford her. She wanted to be happy and he was her happiness.

I love you, I love you, I love you, I love you! She wanted to holler over the cheese omelet and toast, but for the first time, fear was a hindrance.

Reggie slid the cooked omelet from the frying pan to the plate in front of Maya. "I hope you're hungry," he said.

"I'm famished!"

As he turned back toward the stove, Maya admired the denim jeans and loose belt that hung nicely off his ass. His bare back was broad and strong and…

He turned around and smiled at her. "Eat up," he said.

She picked up her fork. "Are you going to join me?"

"Not hungry. I'll eat later."

She took a fork full of omelet. "Very good, baby."

"Thanks. When you finish breakfast, let's get dressed. I have some place I want to take you."

"Where?"

"It's a surprise."

Maya scuffed down her breakfast and darted her naked ass up the stairs to the shower.

Two hours later, as they walked arm and arm out of his palatial estate, Reggie and Maya are greeted by a white stretch limousine. Maya stared blankly with an opened mouth. Reggie looked at his ravishing woman.

"Love, you may want to close your mouth. There are big ass flies here in Orlando," he chuckled.

Maya playfully swatted him on the arm. "What is this, Reggie?"

"Part of my surprise. Now, let's get in because we're running behind."

Maya strolled toward the limousine as the chauffer opened the rear door. She climbed inside and slid to the other side of the car, allowing Reggie to slide in beside her. As the door closed,

Maya tried not to look around in astonishment but she couldn't help it.

"The last time I was in a limousine was at my brother-in-law's funeral," she said, as the vehicle pulled away from the palatial home and down the rock-studded driveway and into the cul-de-sac, which was privately owned by Reggie.

"I promise this occasion will be a happy one," he said, pulling her in close to him and kissing her on the back of the neck.

"Whew, Lord," she squealed as chills ran up and down her back; the hair on the nape of neck stood straight up as if she'd stuck her finger in an electrical outlet.

"You like that, huh?"

She shook her head and moaned, "Uh huh." The hem of the yellow floral print sundress she wore eased above her knee, resting midway on her luscious thighs.

Again, he kissed her neck, that spot directly behind her ear. Her spot. That same spot that always caused her legs to open like an automatic door. That same spot that triggers the gushing dam within her vagina.

She shivered and cooed. He was driving her crazy and he knew it. When she softly blew out air through her pursed lips, he blew his warm breath inside her ear.

"Alright now. You're going to get yourself in some deep trouble, mister."

His large hands took her face gently. The mere touch of his hand sent a warming shiver through her. He softly pressed his lips against her berry-glossed lips. Before his tongue could break though to frolic with hers, he pulled back slightly and looked her longingly in the eyes for what seemed like an eternity. Maya wanted him to take her and the prolonged anticipation was almost unbearable.

"How would it make you feel if I told you I loved you?" he asked, the sweetness of his breath fanning her face.

"Well, I…" she paused as tears of excitement flooded her eyes. She took a deep breath. "I won't know until you tell me."

He kissed her again, his lips still wet and warm. He kissed her cheek. He kissed her ear. He kissed her hot spot, lingering with his tongue. He roamed back to her ear and whispered, "I love you."

"I love you, too," she cooed, and finally felt a bottomless peace and satisfaction. For the first time in her life, she knew how it felt to be genuinely loved by a man.

"Maya, Maya, my sweet, sweet Maya," he whispered, and she tingled as he said her name. "Sweet, sweet baby, I love you so much."

He swept her under him. Her legs instantly wrapped around him and her pulse quickened at the anticipation of him pleasing her. He rubbed up and down her thigh and around her buttocks. She was without panties and it drove him crazy! His fingers roamed like a baby bird heading home, wiggling inside the warmth of its nest until it found that perfect spot to linger. Feeling the electricity of his touch, her body heaved beneath him as his mouth devoured hers. As he rubbed her engorged knot, her body heaved with waves of ecstasy, shivering as if she were standing in the cold naked. He knew her body all too well. She was ready to explode.

"Let it go," he said, followed by her medley of deep-throated moans. "Yes, that's it, baby."

Her legs drew tighter around his waist, her body shook feverishly. "Oh my…I'm about to come," she moaned. She relaxed every muscle in her body, giving in to the passion rushing through her like a tidal wave likened to that of a tsunami ready to crash against land. She yelled out with an erotic pleasure that could be heard for miles. She exploded the floodgates of Dam Maya and crashed against his black, silk shirt.

"Wow, babe! That was a big one."

"Yes," she said, faintly out of breath. "It was massive." She savored the feeling of satisfaction he left with her. "I am totally spent," she admitted.

He chuckled. "I guess you are. Here, let me help you sit up."

Between her legs felt icky as she looked around for napkins or something to wipe herself.

Reggie pulled his shirt out of his pants. "Here, babe, use this," he said, extending the tail of his shirt for her to use.

"Uh, no, I'll be alright. I can use the bathroom at…where are we going again?"

"I'm not telling you, but I can tell you that it'll take us another three hours to get there."

"Three hours! Reggie, where on earth—"

He pressed his finger against her lips. "Hush now, and don't you worry your pretty little head. Trust me, you'll love it!"

He reached across the seat and opened the mini refrigerator. He retrieved a chilled bottle of Moscato d'Asti. After popping the cork, he poured two glasses to the rim.

"Oooh, baby, that's enough."

"There are four more bottles in the fridge and we have three hours to drink it all," he smiled.

Three hours later, the black limousine pulled up to the Hyatt Regency Bonaventure in Weston, Florida.

Maya was curled up, nestled peacefully under Reggie's underarm.

He shook her a bit. "Hey, sweetheart, we're here," he whispered in her ear. "Come on, baby, wake up."

After four bottles of Moscato d'Asti, Maya was fucked up. Reggie was humored as he wiped the dried dribble from the corners of her mouth.

She wiped the corners of her eyes. "Where are we?"

"We're here."

The chauffer opened the door. Reggie got out and extended his hand toward Maya. As she scooted across the seat, a gentle breeze smacked her in the face. She grabbed hold of his hand and stood up out of the car, her knees wobbly, and her balance completely off.

She leaned into to him. "Babe, I am fucked up," she whispered.

"You're fine. Just hold on tight to my arm."

Reggie led her inside the lobby toward the concierge. "Reservations for Reggie Hamilton."

"Yes, Mr. Hamilton, everything is all set for you. If you'll follow me."

"Okay, baby, this is where we part."

She looked confused. "Where are you going?"

"Don't worry, baby. This lovely lady will take very good care of you and I'll see you later. I have a few things I have to take care of."

"But, Reggie…"

"Maya, go, baby. Enjoy yourself today. I love you." He kissed her on the cheek and was off.

"Ms. Howard, if you would follow me, please."

How did she know my name? Maya shrugged it off and followed the thin fair-skinned, dark-haired woman with an uncanny resemblance to Angelina Jolie.

Maya was escorted through double red doors and greeted by yet another thin, fair-skinned woman, but she looked like no one in particular, very average.

"Welcome to the Red Door Lifestyle Spa, Ms. Howard. Mr. Hamilton has taken care of everything," she smiled, pointing to a young lady standing behind her. "This is Kathy, and she will take good care of you for the next five hours."

Damn, five hours? "Can you please tell me exactly what I'll be doing for five hours?"

"Of course. Mr. Hamilton has scheduled you for our Deluxe Package, which includes a Swedish massage and Essential facial, a warm cream manicure and pedicure, a makeover and hair pampering."

Instantly, she became overwhelmed with excitement. She'd never had a massage before nor had she been pampered, and she was ready, set, go!

"Lead the way, Kathy!"

CHAPTER 22

Several hours later, a bellhop led a refreshed, pampered, and somewhat unrecognizable Maya to the Presidential Suite on the second floor of the Bonaventure Hotel.

As they stepped onto the elevator, the bellhop gave Maya a quick once over and cleared his throat.

Lowering her gaze in confusion, Maya blinked with bafflement. "Excuse me?"

The young bellhop blushed. "My apologies."

"Don't apologize, just tell me what your problem is?"

"Again, my apologies, ma'am. I'm just taken aback by your beauty, that's all." Once again, he cleared his throat in embarrassment.

"Oh, I see," she said, trying to suppress a giggle. "Thank you."

"I didn't mean to offend you, ma'am."

"No offense taken, and don't call me ma'am. I ain't that old," she said, her words likened to her favorite scene in *The Color Purple* when Ms. Celie referred to Shug Avery as "Ma'am," and Shug Avery said, "Don't call me ma'am. I ain't that old." She had to chuckle to herself. She absolutely loved that movie, and had to make a note to share that with Reggie. As much time as they've spent together, she didn't know his favorite movie, but she knew his favorite position in bed and how to make his toes curl. That was all she needed to know.

As they approached the Presidential Suite, the bellhop tapped lightly on the door.

"Coming," was heard from inside the suite before the door opened. "Wow!" Reggie's mouth opened wide. He smiled at the bellhop and propped his hands on his hips. "Damn, my woman is beautiful. Wouldn't you say so, my man?" Afraid to utter a word from the elevator fiasco, the bellhop simply nodded his head. Reggie reached in his pocket, pulled out a twenty-dollar-bill, and pressed it into the palm of the bellhop's hand. "Thanks for getting her to me safely."

With the nod of the head and a quick "You're welcome," the bellhop disappeared.

Maya sashayed past Reggie and entered the suite, stopping in her tracks. The massive suite stole her breath like a thief in the night.

Reggie threw Maya a long, penetrating look. His loins were on fire and he was ready for her juices to put out the fire, but that had to wait. The plan was laid out and he had to follow it to a tee.

"Beautiful room, isn't it?"

"Oh my goodness, Reggie. I've never seen anything more beautiful."

"I have," he said, walking up behind her. "You, my love, are the most beautiful creature I've ever seen."

Maya flushed inside with happiness as Reggie planted a small kiss on the nape of her neck.

"Oooohwee," she squealed. "You know that's my spot." She faced her man and planted the most loving kiss upon his lips. "Have I told you lately that I love you?"

"Yes, but let me hear it again."

She stared at him with longing. "I love you," she whispered to him, followed by her tongue stroking across his full lips.

She made him weak in the knees and he was about buckle, but he had to be strong if he was going to pull his plan off right.

He patted her backside. "I love you, sweet, sweet baby."

Her hand roamed over his chest and abdomen. He stopped her before she reached his crotch. He took her by the hand and led her toward the dining table, donned with all of her favorite foods that she had never tasted before she'd met him: lobster, caviar, cracked crab, shrimp, and champagne in long-stemmed flutes.

Her eyes bugged out! "Wow, what's all this for, honey?"

"Oh, nothing really. Just wanted to do something special, show you how much I love you. You know, that little stuff," he smiled.

"Well, I love the little stuff!" she giggled, taking her seat.

He took the napkin from the plate, unfolded it, and placed it gently in her lap. He sat across from her and did the same.

"This has been the most wonderful day, baby. I can't thank you enough for all that you've done for me. You make me feel so special, Reggie."

"No need to thank me. You're my woman. That's what a man does for his woman. My goal is to keep you happy." He blew her a kiss, stoking a gently growing fire between her thighs.

Silenced lingered as he watched Maya enjoy her meal. After several moments, she looked up from her plate and into his eyes.

"Why are you staring at me?" she asked him, still chewing on lobster.

He rose from his seat, pulled something from his pocket, and approached her. He knelt down on one knee, took her by the hand, and held up an engagement ring. "Will you marry me?"

She coughed, taken by surprise, and the remaining lobster went down the wrong way.

CHAPTER 23

Atlanta, Georgia

The bowling alley was jammed with youngsters on a Friday night. Colored lights flashed overhead and Bobby Brown's "My Prerogative" was blasting on the oldies but goodies station. Sam watched Free swoop across the bowling alley floor, one leg crossed behind the other, and tossed out her ball. It landed perfectly in the middle of the lane. She stood poised like a statue as it spun and crashed through the ten dirty white pins.

"A strike!" she teased, pumping her fists over her head. "Yeah, boyyyyyy!"

Sam's lip curled up at the corner into a sexy smirk. "Sheer luck."

"It may be luck, but I'm kicking your butt!" she chuckled as she approached him, a little out of breath, and sat on his lap. The sweet smell of Alfred Sung meshed with her body chemistry, delighting his senses. He felt his bulge growing. Free must've felt it, too. She wiggled her ass. "Somebody's getting excited," she said in sing-song fashion.

Sam moved her braids to the side and kissed the back of her neck, sending a bolt of chills throughout her.

"Whew, alright now," she said eyeballing the bowling alley, "you gon' get yourself in trouble messing with me."

"Punish me, baby," he said, kissing her again on the neck and grabbing her breast.

She swatted his hand away. "Samuel!"

He squeezed her thigh as he slid out from under her, taking her by the hand. "Let's go."

"But we're not finished bowling."

"Oh, yes we are." Sam led her out into the night toward his red Jaguar parked in the crowded parking lot. He opened the back door. "After you, milady."

Since dating Sam, Free had learned to throw caution to the wind and enjoy the ride. So far, so good, but she was a little leery about the backseat and a crowded parking lot. She slid into the car and Sam slid in behind her and closed the door.

Free looked down at her feet. "What about the shoes?"

"What about them?"

"Uh, they belong to the bowling alley, Sam!"

Sam patted his thighs. "Put your feet up here."

Giggling, she plopped her feet upon his lap. He untied the laces and pulled off each shoe. He opened the door and tossed them out of the car.

"What'd you do that for?"

"I'm giving them back their shoes."

Free fell out with laughter. "You have issues. Now what about *my* shoes?"

He held her foot up to his mouth and kissed her big toe. "I'll replace them," he said, covering her big toe with his mouth.

Ewwwwwwwwwwwww! "Now, that's nasty, Sam. I'm not kissing you!"

"Come here, woman." He pulled her in close to him. "Have I told you how much you turn me on?"

"I'm listening."

He kissed her on the cheek. "You have no idea what you do to me, woman." He kissed her on the ear. She shivered. His fingers played with the button on her shirt until it gave way to his persistency. The warmth of his strong hand caressed her soft breast as he took her hardened nipple inside his mouth.

Free moaned with pleasure, her insides burning like a raging fire. Sam had that effect on her.

Leaving her nipple, his mouth feverishly covered hers. He slid his hands between her soft fleshy belly and the elastic waistband of her cotton stretch pants. He inhaled deeply, taking her breath and intoxicating her.

She moaned deeply as his fingers played in her pubic hair, twisting and pulling, before ever so gently stroking her thick vagina lips.

Ignoring the hustle and bustle of patrons entering and leaving the parking lot, Free rotated her hips against Sam's hand, allowing his fingers to slip inside her wetness.

"Oooh, baby," he cooed. "I want some pussy." She loved it when he talked dirty. "Can I have some of your sweet pussy, baby?" She nodded her head, but that wasn't enough for Sam. "Can I, baby? Huh? You gon' let me have some of my sweet pussy?" He gently pinched her swollen clitoris.

"Yes," she moaned.

"Feed me that pussy, baby."

She raised her hips, pulled her pants down around her ankles, and slipped them off. When she opened her legs, her sweet aroma wafted up into Sam's nostrils and he went fool crazy. He yanked her down in the seat and spread her legs—one foot nestled in the back window, pressed against the glass, and the other resting on the armrest between the driver and passenger seat in the front. The old Free would have been mortified at her behavior. The new Free wanted Sam's dick every chance she could get it.

Quickly, Sam maneuvered his pants down around his ankles and hoisted one leg up over Free's head, planting his knee deep in the seat. His erection stroked her lips and, like the doors of McDonald's on a busy Saturday night, her mouth opened and allowed him entry. It was the most uncomfortable sixty-nine she had ever encountered, but she wasn't going to let a little discomfort and Sam's musty balls in her face keep her from pleasing her man. Free sucked that fat tootsie roll determined to taste the saltiness in the middle while he devoured her pussy. Sam had her lips spread so far apart. He licked every nook and cranny hurriedly, wanting to bring her to full climax. He loved her oral skills, but the ache to slide inside her was unbearable.

"Come for me, baby," he said as his index finger rhythmically tapped her clitoris.

Free felt like she was going to explode. The unexplainable feeling building inside her was overwhelming. She was like a shaken soda bottle and she couldn't hold it any longer. Of course, Sam knew his woman better than she knew herself. When she was ready for blastoff, her inner thighs would heat up as though someone had taken a match to them and tremble like the aftermath of a Los Angeles earthquake. He knew exactly what to do. He took his index finger and pulled back the hood of her clitoris, exposing the most sensitive part of a woman's body, and vigorously stroked the soft, fleshy glands with his tongue. There she blows! Free moaned from deep within and squirted in Sam's face and all over the backseat.

As her body trembled with pleasure and not wanting to be touched, Sam flipped himself around and quickly inserted his throbbing manhood inside her. She was tight, the skin of his head pulled back, giving a tad bit of pain. But it was that good pain he loved to feel when stroking his woman. Within minutes and after several quick humps, Sam's body stiffened and her legs wrapped around his waist, ensuring he would not slip out of her. His face distorted, which she loved to watch, and the noise that came from within him was like a wounded animal. She released her vaginal muscles, taking in every single drop of his seeds.

"Goddamn, baby, whew!" He looked down at her. "Baby," he shook his head, "you've got some good ass pussy."

There was a time when Free would have taken such talk as being vulgar and gutter-like, but Sam had peeled back the layers of her bitter onion, revealing a one hundred percent freak.

Her head was spinning and her body felt wonderful; however, one thought ran rampant through her mind: No condom and no diaphragm.

Damn it!

CHAPTER 24

The next morning, air rushed across the opened sun roof. Andre occupied the passenger seat while Ashley, covered from head to toe with a Miami Dolphin velvet throw, took over the backseat stretched out. She slept the entire eight-hour drive. Shifting down to second gear, China turned right onto Sycamore Driving in Atlanta before pulling into Free's driveway.

China playfully popped Andre upside the head. "Alright, my man. We're here." She looked in the rearview mirror. "Ashley, wake up, honey. We're at Aunt Free's house."

From her bed, she heard a car pull into the driveway. She rose up out of bed and walked barefoot toward the window. Her feet slapped against the chilly hardwood floor. She pulled back the curtain and couldn't believe her eyes. "China?" She hurried to the closet for her robe, rushed out of the bedroom and down the staircase, and flung open the front door.

"Surprise!" China yelled with Andre and Ashley flanked on both sides. It was six o'clock in the morning.

"Hey, sis!" Free hugged China and then the children. "You two go upstairs and get some sleep. You look like the walking dead. Ashley, you can take your Aunt Maya's room, and Andre, you take the other spare room."

Ashley and Andre rushed past their Aunt Free and made a beeline to grab a few hours of shuteye.

"Girl, I'm exhausted, too," China said, walking past Free and dropping her bags in the foyer. "I would love a cup of coffee."

"Sure, come on in the kitchen. You hungry, too?"

"I could use a little something to eat."

Hot coffee was a morning ritual for Free, so the automatic brewer was ready to brew. She pushed the on switch and shuffled toward the refrigerator. She pulled out a carton of eggs, bacon, cheese, tomatoes, onions, mushrooms, and chili peppers. She sat the ingredients on the granite countertop and faced China, who had taken a seat at the kitchen table.

"This is truly a surprise, sis. I wasn't expecting you. Why didn't you tell me you were coming?"

Feeling on edge after the long drive and irritation rose in her throat, China pushed out, "I didn't know I had to make reservations to come see my sister."

"No, not at all, you're always welcome. It's just a surprise, that's all." Free continued moving about the kitchen, preparing breakfast, and pouring coffee.

China got up and opened the refrigerator. "Got any of that flavored cream that I like?"

"Yep, on the side of the door, toward the bottom." Free sat two cups of coffee on the table and pulled up a seat. She waited for China to sit across from her before she spoke. Peering at her sister, she knew something was wrong. It was written all over her face. The dark circles under her eyes were as prominent as her graying roots that were long overdue for Dark & Lovely. She looked exhausted, defeated, and it damn near broke Free's heart. "Honey, what's wrong?"

China shrugged her shoulders. "It was time to go."

"What do you mean? Did something happen?"

"I put the house on the market. The memories of Ron are too much. The bloodstains are still in the bedroom carpet, Free." Her voice quivered and her eyes welled.

Free reached across the table and grabbed her hands. "Honey, it's going to be okay. You and the kids can stay here for as long as you want."

"Thank you, sis."

"So, you're going to sell the house, huh?"

China nodded.

"Selling the house isn't going to rid you of the memories, China."

"Maybe not, but at least I won't be wallowing in them."

"You said there are bloodstains on the carpet?"

"Well, not anymore. I had the carpet replaced yesterday, before we left. My realtor thinks the house is going to go fast. "

With that said Free stood up and wiped her hands on her robe. "How about a Western Omelet?"

"Sounds delicious…with chili peppers?"

"Of course."

China smiled. "Where's Maya?"

"In Orlando."

"Again?"

"Yep. He sends for her just about every weekend."

"Wow. Well, I'm happy for her."

Free's mouth flew open. "What'd you say?"

"She's my sister. I may not like her all the time, but I do love her and care about what happens to her."

Free rushed to the kitchen door and looked out at the sky.

"What're you doing?" asked China.

"Checking to see if the sky is falling."

"Ha! Funny."

"Hey, I know what you need."

"Ut oh, I'm scared to ask, but I'll take a chance. What do I need?"

"A man!"

"How do you figure I need a man?"

"What are you going to do? Grieve for the rest of your life?" Free asked, scrambling the omelet mixture and pouring it into the hot buttered pan.

China shook her head. "No, not ready to date yet. In fact, I don't ever want to date, get married again, none of that shit. I can't take any more pain."

"Oh, China, don't give up on life."

"Honey, life gave up on me when my man fucked another man and then blew his damn brains out."

Free spun around and stared helplessly at her sister. She had always known how to fix her sisters' lives, but she couldn't repair a broken heart. A tear welled in her eye. She wiped it away just as it was about to fall. She turned her attention back to the task of preparing breakfast and pulled two plates down from the cupboard. Silence draped the kitchen as Free plated breakfast and placed the plates delicately on the table. She slowly took a seat, as if her legs would give way, and slid a plate in front of China.

"Just the way you like it," Free said, slightly smiling.

China glared into her sister's eyes. What she needed was one of Free's motherly hugs, not a Western omelet.

As if reading her thoughts, Free stood, walked around to the other side of the table, and caressed China's shoulders, kissing her on the cheek.

China buried her face in Free's arm and cried. For the first time since Ron's death, she felt safe and secure with her big sister Free. Then, she gathered herself and wiped her nose on the sleeve of her arm and looked at the Western Omelet. Her face twisted as if she was in agony.

Free stood erect. "What's wrong?"

"How am I to eat? With my hands?"

Free glanced at the table. "Oh, sorry. Forgot the forks," she chuckled.

"Being forgetful comes with age, you know," retorted China.

The both chuckled and enjoyed Free's special Western Omelet.

They sat at opposite ends of the sofa sipping Long Island Iced Teas.

"Something I've been meaning to ask you, China."

"Yeah? What's that?"

"The second test…how did it go?"

China looked at Free and smiled. "Negative."

"Thank the good Lord," said Free.

"Yes." China smiled and nodded her head in agreement. "Thank the good Lord. I couldn't imagine having to leave my babies without a mother."

"Girl, don't even think like that!" exclaimed Free.

China kicked off her shoes and propped her feet on top of the ottoman and reclined her head.

"You need to start dating."

China rolled her eyes, slightly irritated with the whole topic of her needing a man. She'd thought they had gone over that earlier that morning and the topic should have been dead and stinking. But leave it to Free to bring it up, yet again.

"Free, I'm not interested in dating nobody."

"China, how long will you sit around being miserable?"

"I'm not miserable."

"You sure look it. You have a permanent ugly scowl on your face."

The television was off, but China stared at it. She pondered deeply on Free's words. She knew Free was right, but she thought it was absurd for a widower to start prowling months after burying a spouse, and she simply wasn't going to do it.

"Free, let it go, please."

"I know how you feel—"

"No, you don't know how I feel, which is why you should let… it…go."

"Look, you're a healthy woman. Don't you crave a man?"

China sipped the last of her drink and held it out to Free. "Aren't you on drink detail? Plus, I have a silver bullet."

Free hissed, took the glass, and disappeared into the kitchen. "Your stuff is going to fall off if you keep using that thing!" she shouted into the living room.

China responded with a chuckle. She knew Free only wanted the best for her, but she simply wasn't ready. When the time was right, she would begin to date again. But she wondered when that time would come. While she loved her silver bullet, she did crave the touch of a man. She'd been reading enough erotica novels to keep her masturbating for years to come.

Returning to her seat on the sofa, Free sat China's glass on the table. "You and that doggone silver thing. Girl, that bullet ain't gon' hold you at night or kiss you or love you…"

"It makes my pussy explode and that's all I need for now. Thank you very much."

"Wow!" Free looked at China in astonishment with her mouth gaped opened. "That's just nasty."

China repositioned herself, sitting on one leg and facing Free. "Listen, honey, I know you mean well. I really do, but, baby, when the time is right…or better yet, when it is in God's plans, I'll meet someone."

Free relaxed her posture. "You're right," smiled Free. "I guess—"

"I have to make sure my shit is in order before I go looking for someone. I have to make sure that whatever I want dude to bring to the table that I can do the same. Do you know what I mean?"

"Yes, I know, and I'm sorry for being so pushy."

"It's alright, sis. I know your heart is in the right place."

Free sipped her refreshed drink. "So, what are your plans?"

"Well, I want to be closer to my family. So, I'm going to move back home."

"Really, China? Oh, that is wonderful. When are you planning to make that move?"

"I just did."

Free's brows furrowed. "What do you mean?"

"Oh, I didn't tell you?" China chuckled and stretched her legs and arms out in front of her. "Girl, I had an estate sale last week and sold every stitch of everything in my house. From the furniture down to Ron's clothes."

The shock of discovery hit Free full force. "You sold everything?"

"Yep, even Ron's car sold quickly, too."

"Wait. You sold Ron's vintage Mustang?"

China nodded. "Yes, ma'am, and guess who I sold it to?"

"Who?" she said eagerly.

"Marion!"

"No!"

"Yes!"

"But I thought you didn't want to have anything to do with him?"

"I don't, but his money is legal tender, too."

"But how did he know you were selling the car?"

"He saw the ad I placed in the paper about the estate sale."

Free smirked and folded her arms over her breast. "Humph, I'm surprised you sold it to him."

"Yeah, me too, actually. But it is what it is."

"Change of attitude…I like that, China."

"Yeah, I guess. Anyway, I'm here to stay. The only reason I'll go back to Orlando is to collect the money from the sale of the house, which, I might add, is paid in full, baby!"

Free was baffled. *How can that be*, she wondered.

As if reading Free's thoughts, China said, "We had that special insurance on the house, that if anything happened to either one of us, the house would be paid in full. That's the one good thing that son of a bitch did for his family."

"Really? I need to check into that myself."

China raised her hand. "Hold tight, sister. If you and Sam get married, I wouldn't put his name on this house. Put it in someone else's name."

"Why wouldn't I put my *husband's name* on my house?"

"Because your *husband* didn't lift one hand nor pitch in one penny to buy this house, did he? And, he's not your *husband* yet."

"Well, no, but…never mind. I'll cross that bridge when I get to it, and that is something I'll discuss with Sam when he becomes my *husband*."

"Speaking of, what are you going to do about the shop? Are you going to rebuild?"

"Yes, thank God for insurance. Hey, so you're going to be staying with me, right?"

"Well, no, we can grab a hotel room—"

"Grab a what? Nonsense. You and the kids can stay here."

"Are you sure it's going to be okay? I mean, Free, you already have Maya's freeloading ass here and I'm sure we'll get on Sam's nerves."

"Hush, it'll be fine," Free said, although deep in the back of her mind she knew having China and Maya under the same roof would be toxic. But she was willing to deal with it. "So, this means you can go with me and Jade to Los Angeles this weekend."

"Oh, that's right…Will Maya be back then? The kids can stay here with her."

"Well, I don't know. Maya seems to be on a plane every single weekend going to see Reggie."

China twisted up her mouth. "You know, I'm glad she finally found someone to love."

Free snapped her head in the direction of China. She couldn't believe her ears. "What did you just say?"

"Yeah, I know, but dealing with Ron's death…well, the stubbornness is slowly subsiding, I suppose."

Free smiled. "Yeah, I suppose. But, look, if Maya isn't able to watch them, then I'm sure Sam won't mind—"

"Yeah," China blurted. "Since he lives here!"

"Chile, please, Sam does not live here."

China stared wordlessly at Free before leaving her seat and darting up the stairs like a bat out of hell.

"Where are you going?" Free yelled after her.

China bolted into Free's bedroom making a beeline to her closet. She flung the double doors open. "Ah hah!" she yelled at the top of her lungs.

Still on the sofa, Free buried her face in her hands and took a deep sigh.

"I thought you said he didn't live her," China yelled from inside Free's walk-in closet.

Free remained silent, but she smiled and thought, *That wench makes me sick*, followed by a soft chuckle.

China's footsteps plowed down the stairs, barreling into the living room. She stood before Free with her hands on her hips. "You weren't fooling me for one second, wanna be Ms. Goody-Two-Shoes!"

Free broke into laughter. "Mind your own business. Sam does not live here."

"His clothes are in your closet."

"So?"

"So? That means he lives here."

"No, it does not. He has his own place. He's only here on the weekends."

"Really now," China said sarcastically, folding her arms across her chest.

"Yes, really," Free mocked.

"Today is Wednesday."

Free stood up and stretched her arms high above her head before picking up the glasses from the coffee table. "And your point is what?"

"It smells like he was here last night."

"What? Okay, now I know you've lost your mind."

"Your room smells like his cologne and pussy!"

"China! I swear, your mouth!"

China laughed hysterically. "It's not the weekend, slut," China said, playfully popping Free on the behind. "With your hot ass."

Free faced China and, as much as she wanted to, she could not contain it. A smile crept across her face and they both fell out with laughter.

"Well, nonetheless, he'll be here this weekend and he can watch Ashley and Andre, if you don't have a problem with him doing so?"

"Oh, no, not at all. I think Sam's real cool," she said, following Free into the kitchen. "But now I have to go shopping."

"For what?"

"I sold all of my clothes."

"Now why would you do that?"

"Because I'm greedy. Hell, do you know how much money I raised last week?"

Free looked at her and slightly shook her head.

"Well, dear sister, I raised enough money to live on for the next ten years without having to get a job!"

"Go 'way from here!"

"Yep. Ron's 1965 Mustang Convertible sold for $75,000."

"Seventy-five..." Free trailed off in complete shock. "Now, China, I don't know a thing about cars, but I can almost assure you that car is probably worth no more than $10,000."

"You're probably right, but that's what Marion wanted to pay for it."

"Wow, that's...um, I just don't know what to say about it."

"I say that guilt is a son of a bitch!"

"I guess so. Well since you told me how much the car sold for—"

"Girl, he gave me cash, too!"

"Yeah?"

"Uh huh. It seems like Ron's ass buddy owns several hair salons throughout the Orlando area and a couple in Miami. Well, that explains it though."

"Explains what?"

"Why he liked digging around in my man's ass."

"Oh, China, just when I thought you were starting to change, here you go with this mess. Do you know how ignorant you sound?"

"Sometimes the truth can sound ignorant."

Free shook her head in disgust and changed the subject. "Well, if you're going shopping, you better hop to it. We're leaving Friday morning. I guess I should call Jade and let her know that you're going with us. It'll be so much fun!"

"Hey, Free, don't call her. Let's surprise her. I need to get on the phone and get my plane ticket though."

Free shook her head. "No, you don't. We're flying first class, compliments of Mr. Jon Meadows."

"Really now? Well alright, let me take myself to Lenox Square. You coming?"

"No, you go ahead. Enjoy yourself!"

China grabbed her purse from the kitchen counter and called out to Ashley. "Let's roll, girlie!"

Ashley rushed down the stairs and met her mother in the foyer. "Where are we going, Mom?"

"To the mall to do a little shopping," she said in sing-song fashion with a huge smile. She loved shopping with her daughter.

At the top of the staircase, Andre was bobbing over the railing, trying to see what the ruckus was all about. "What's up, Mom?"

"None of your business," Ashley shot back.

"Stop being so mean to your brother," China said, popping her upside the head. "Going to Lenox Square. Would you like to come with us?" she asked, rolling her eyes at Ashley, followed by a warm, motherly smile.

"For shizzle, my—"

"Your what?" China snapped. "What did I tell you about using that language?"

Andre drug himself down the steps with slouching shoulders. "Aw, Mom, you need to get up with the times, babe."

With one hand on her hip, China tilted her head to the side and glared at Andre. "Listen, young man, I am not your babe, baby, hoochie, or none of that other mess you hear on those rap songs or on music videos," China huffed. "Respect your mother, boy, before I whip your ass the next time."

Andre winked at his mother and said "Yes, Mom, but you'll always be my girl," followed by a heart laughter that was warm and genuine.

China looked at him with amused wonder. "I swear I think they switched babies the day you were born," she said, smiling as she opened the front door and stepped back for her offspring to exit. "Be back in a little while, Free," she called out, closing the door behind her.

CHAPTER 25

A s the Volvo S80 idled in the driveway, China looked in the rearview mirror at the yellow taxi cab pulling up behind her.

"What are we waiting for, Ma?" asked Andre.

China turned her attention to the side view mirror to see a pair of voluptuous bare legs exit the back of the cab.

"I'm waiting to say hello to Aunt Maya."

"Oh, that's my girl," Andre chuckled.

Keeping her attention on Maya taking her sweet time climbing out of the cab, China extended her arm and introduced the back of her hand to Andre's mouth.

"Owwww!"

"Don't be disrespectful. That's your aunt."

"That's what you get!" Ashley teased.

"My arm can extend to the back just as easily, Ms. Ashley."

"Ha!" Andre retorted.

"Shut up!" Ashley whined.

"No, you shut up!"

"You both shut the hell up!" China snapped, rolling down the car window. She stuck out her arm and waved at Maya. "Hey, sis!"

Surprisingly excited to see her sister, Maya tipped the cab driver and rushed toward China's car. "Hey, girl. What are y'all doing here?" She looked inside the car. "Hello, my babies," she greeted, blowing Ashley and Andre invisible kisses.

"Hi, Aunt Maya," they greeted in unison.

"We're here for good," China said. "We're going to Lenox Square, want to go with us?"

"Naw, I'm exhausted. Just getting back from Orlando, and what do you mean you're here for good?"

"Ask Free, she'll fill you in. I'll see you lata, gata."

"After while, crocodile," retorted Maya, leaving the car and jogging up to the front door.

"Geesh, how corny was that?" said Ashley.

"Hush, girl. You don't know a thing about that," China smiled as she put the car in drive and slowly pulled away from the curb.

Free saw Maya coming toward the house and opened the front door for her.

"Thanks, honey. I just saw China," Maya said, dropping her bags to the floor and giving Free a big hug.

Free's eyes widened in shock. "You're welcome, and yeah it looks like she's going to stay for good." *Well, she needs to go to Florida more often.*

"Yeah? That's good to hear," Maya said, and Free looked at her like she'd lost her mind. Maya's response simply was not typical of one pertaining to China.

"So, how was your trip?"

"As usual, it was relaxing."

"How's Reggie?"

"He's good," she smiled. "Now I need to take a hot bath," she said, picking up her bags and heading up the stairs to her bedroom.

"Oh, by the way, you and Ashley will have to share a room. Is that okay with you?"

"Yes, that's fine," Maya said gleefully.

"Are you sure?"

"Uh huh, yeah, I'm sure."

"Okay, now," Free said, following Maya up the stairs. "What's going on with you?"

Maya tossed her bags on the bed and faced Free. "Nothing, why do you ask?" She kicked off her Coach wedge heels.

"Because normally you would break into a hissy fit if I told you that you had to share your room."

Maya shrugged her shoulders, smiled, and pulled her shirt over her head. "I really don't mind," she said, tossing it onto the bed. "I can bond with my niece."

Still amazed at Maya's reaction, Free sat down on the bed. "So, tell me something good," she said, poking around in Maya's bags. "I know you brought back something good. You always do."

Maya spun around and held up her left hand. "I'm engaged!" She shouted out the good news, flashing a four-carat, heart-shaped diamond and blue sapphire ring on her engagement finger. "Reggie asked me last night and I said yes, yes, YES!"

Free jumped to her feet. "I am so happy for you," she said, giving her a big hug. "You deserve to be happy, Maya, but..."

Maya spun around in a circle, but came to a screeching halt. "But what?"

"But...you just met him. You don't know him. This is kind of fast, isn't it?" Free looked down at Maya's stomach.

Maya clutched her belly. "I am not pregnant!"

A sigh of relief graced Free's face. The last thing Maya needed was a baby when she could barely take care of herself. "I'm just saying, Maya..."

"We're in love, Free." Joy radiated on her face and shone in her eyes. "Reggie is the best thing that has ever happened to me. Don't you understand? He loves me, sis."

"So," Free said, standing like a motherly figure with her hands propped on her hips. "When will your family get to meet this wonderful man of yours?"

"This weekend! He's flying here on Friday, and—" The shaking of Free's head stopped her in her tracks. "What?"

"We're going to Los Angeles this weekend, remember?"

Maya's shoulders slouched and her bottom lip damn near hit the floor.

Spoiled ass brat! Free thought, rolling her eyes. "What about the following weekend?" she asked, offering a resolution to a problem she simply didn't want to do deal with—Maya's whining.

Maya's eyes lit up. "Okay, that'll work. I'm sure Reggie wouldn't mind. I'll call him later." Maya returned to the task of putting away her things when she realized she was, once again, being excluded. She neatly folded her panties and tucked them in her undergarment drawer. "When you say we, Free, who are you referring to?"

Ut oh. . . "Me, Jade, and China..." Free paused, waiting for Storm Maya to ensue.

"Really? Wow... Okay, well, um...I can't believe—"

"Why don't you come with us?"

Maya's heart sang with delight when she said, "I'd love to come!"

"Great," Free said, forcing a smile. *China and Jade are going to kill me,* she thought, leaving Maya's room.

CHAPTER 26

Free felt a lump in her throat when she stood on the tarmac of Hartsfield Jackson Airport, waiting for Jon*Air* to arrive. She was terrified as she'd never been that close to so many big ass planes before. "They look so small in the sky," she mumbled to herself.

China overheard her. "What are you talking about?"

Free shook her head. "Nothing." Although terrified, this time she would put her fear of flying to the side. Since it was Jon's private plane, she felt a little more at ease.

The wind was brisk as Maya held a compact mirror in one hand and a tube of lipstick in the other. Grit and grime kicked up, meshing with the N.Y.C. mocha lip paint across her lips.

"Are you sure Sam won't mind keeping an eye on the kids?" China asked Free, rummaging through her bag, pulling out a pair of sunglasses. "I mean, you know, I don't want to be a burden." She put on the shades and looked up in the air. "Where the hell is that plane and why do we have to stand out here?"

Free sighed. "Which question do you want me to answer first, honey?"

Maya chuckled.

"Look, I just don't want to impose, that's all."

"China, Sam is fine. Ashley and Andre are going to be fine. Okay?"

Maya pointed upward. "Is that it?"

"I think so," replied Free. "That sure is a tiny plane."

"Yeah, tiny as shit." China looked around them. "How much luggage do we have?"

"Why?" asked Maya.

"Because those little ass planes can only carry but so much weight or else we'll go down in a ball of fire. SPLAT! Just like that," she said, clapping her hands together, knowing darn well Free was terrified of flying. "SPLAT! SPLAT! SPLAT!" she said with each clap of her hands.

"Shut the hell up, China!" Free barked, now more nervous than she was five minutes ago.

China laughed, Maya giggled, and Free hissed.

Jon*Air* touched down and Maya grabbed up her bags. "Here we go, that's it!"

China swung her duffle bag over her shoulder and pulled up close to Maya, looping arms with her. Maya looked down at China's arm, then up at her face. China smiled. *What the fuck is going on?* Maya thought, actually feeling uncomfortable. Having her sister so close up under her wasn't the norm, especially looped arm-in-arm like they had some kind of wonderful relationship and were ready to skip down the Yellow Brick Road. The closest China had ever gotten to her was when she tried to kill her at a family reunion.

Free couldn't believe her eyes either. Things seemed to have been changing for the better. She wasn't complaining though. Maybe China's behavior was a sign that all would be peaches and cream over the weekend.

Then, Maya stood erect. "Oh my, God," she whispered.

"What's wrong?" asked China, looking Maya in the face.

"Oh no," she whispered and looked at China. "I can't go to Los Angeles. They'll arrest me."

"Girl, hush, they don't even know who you are. Besides, they probably don't give a rat's ass about a pimp being killed. Good ridden to that piece of trash."

Free overheard China and Maya. In the back of her mind, she also wondered if Maya's traveling to Los Angeles wasn't such a good idea after all. But, she pushed the thought in the back of her mind as life had to go on. If it was meant to be, then Maya would have no choice but to confront and deal head on with the consequences, with her sisters supporting her one hundred percent.

"It's been almost a year, Maya. If they don't know who you are by now or haven't come looking for you, then I wouldn't worry about it."

Maya nodded, yet she was still feeling uneasy. However, maybe Free was right. It had been almost a year since she rammed a broom handle down Jonah's well-deserving throat. Did she mean to kill him? Yes, and she would've chopped him up into tiny little pieces and flushed his ass down the toilet if it were in her to do so.

As Jon*Air* taxied to the gate, Free moved backward as close to the terminal as possible without causing herself any danger.

China turned around and looked at Free, determined that her sister had lost her mind. "What are you doing, girl? Come on!"

"It doesn't look like its going to stop," Free yelled over the loud hum of the plane's engine.

When the leer jet came to a halt, Free moved in a little closer, pulling up behind an anxious Maya and China.

"Not as small as I thought it would be," yelled China, as the hatch door opened to unfolding steps.

Jade appeared in the doorway of Jon*Air*. "Hello, sisters! Come on aboard."

"Hey, Jade," Free called out, waving. "Hey!"

"Okay, Ms. Celie," China said to Free, laughing.

"Oh hush," Free said, shoving her.

"I have to pee," said Maya.

"You always have to pee," snapped China.

They hurried toward the plane with their bags in tow.

"No, leave your bags down there. The crew will take care of them."

China, Free, and Maya looked at each other and dropped their bags to the ground. "A crew?" Maya mumbled. "Well ain't this here some shit."

"Don't start," Free said, pushing her up the steps. "I thought you had to pee."

Jade couldn't wait for her sisters to board Jon*Air*, a leer jet personally designed by Jon Meadows and updated by Jade Howard.

Maya was the first to board. "Hey, Jade!" She greeted her sister with a warm smile and big hug, which threw Jade completely off. "I have to pee," she told Jade.

"The bathroom is in the back." A petite brown-skinned woman, holding a tray of flutes filled to the brim with Dom Perignon, stood beside Jade. "This is Veronica, Jon's Personal Assistant. Veronica, this is my sister, Maya." Jade took the tray from Veronica. "Will you please show my sister to the bathroom?"

"Absolutely. Hi, Maya…follow me."

"Hey, y'all!" Jade greeted China and Free, giving them both kisses on the cheek. "Care for a drink?"

"Thank you," China said, taking a flute.

"No thank you," said Free, looking around at the spacious plane that was like nothing she'd ever seen before.

"Take the damn drink, Free," scolded China.

Sighing heavily, Free took the drink to shut China up. If they wanted to be couple of lushes, that was their choice. But she was going to carry herself appropriately.

Following behind Veronica, Maya stroked the headrest of the beige Italian leather seats, trimmed in chocolate brown and soft like butter. There were seven seats: three with flat screen monitors facing the front of the plane, four facing each other—situated to play cards or hold a small meeting—and a love seat. The wall-to-wall beige carpeting blended well with the mocha wood grain paneling.

Veronica opened the door of the bathroom. "Here you are, Maya."

"Thank you," said Maya with her mouth gaped wide opened at the full-sized bathroom with oak paneling, gold-plated fixtures, cream-colored wall-to-wall plush carpeting, and an eight-tier chandelier. A tiny dispenser above the toilet released a fragrance of Patchouli. A basket of complimentary lotions, soaps, mouthwash, toothbrushes, and hand sanitizers sat on the sink.

"I'm sure you'll find everything you need in here," Veronica said, amused at Maya's reaction. *The commoners simply aren't used to such lavishness,* she thought, giggling to herself.

Maya moved inside the bathroom and sat her purse on the floor. "Wow, this is truly unbelievable," she said, dropping her jeans and taking a much needed squat. She'd thought her bladder would pop from holding her pee for so long. A warm mist of water sprayed her bottom. "What the hell? Well ain't that a blip. Damn toilet cleaning your ass," she said, wrapping a stream of toilet paper around her hand and wiping her bottom. As she pulled up her jeans, the toilet automatically flushed, The beautiful scent of Patchouli filled the air, and water flowed from the faucet without her having to touch it. She shook her head, washed her hands, and left to find her sisters.

China and Free sat comfortably in the seats with flat screen televisions, and Jade and Veronica sat opposite each other at the work table.

"Nice, isn't it?" Jade asked Maya, watching her toss her purse on the sofa.

Maya plopped down on the sofa. "Girl, now I could live in that bathroom!"

"It's that nice, huh?" asked Free.

"You have to see it to believe it," Maya said.

The fasten seatbelts light engaged and everyone strapped themselves in.

"We're on our own today, sisters," Jade said. "No flight attendants."

"Yes," Veronica chimed in, "but we certainly have enough food and drink to hold us over." She giggled, tossing Jade a smirk, remembering Jade's first trip aboard Jon*Air*.

That, too, was a day that Jade will never forget. She had just met Jon Meadows days before he kidnapped her and jetted her off to his home in Montego Bay, Jamaica. It was the best weekend of Jade's life and the most memorable.

After Jon*Air* climbed thirty-five thousand feet in the air, Veronica unfastened her seatbelt and stood up. "Anyone care for a glass of champagne?"

"Is it that Don Petey stuff Jade's always drinking?" asked Free.

The plane erupted in laughter.

"Yes," Veronica confirmed. "That's it. How many glasses shall I pour?"

"I'll take one," said China.

"Yep, one for me, too," said Maya.

"You know I want one," said Jade.

"No, thank you, and Jade drinks a whole bottle not a glass," said Free.

China waved her hand at Free. "Veronica, she will have a glass, too. Her uptight ass needs to unwind. We are on our way to Los Angeles and we are going to have a good time this weekend, yes indeedy!"

With a warm smile, Veronica moved toward the front of the plane and entered the mini-sized kitchen that was neatly packed with any and everything one would find in a full-sized kitchen. She grabbed five champagne flutes and placed them on a small tray. Then, she opened the mini refrigerator, removed five bottles of Dom Perignon, and sat them down on the tray. She pulled the latch on the drawer and opened it, retrieving a black and silver corkscrew. Just like a flight attendant, Veronica rolled the cart up the aisle. "Here we are, ladies," she said, handing each one a champagne flute.

Reluctantly, Free took the flute and raised it. "We do have something to toast to," she said, looking at Maya.

"Yes, you're definitely not a drinker. You only raise the glass when there's something in it, you silly!" China said, breaking into laughter.

"Leave Free alone," Jade said, reaching for a bottle and corkscrew. Like a pro, Jade popped the cork and started filling her flute and everyone else's. "So," she said, nestling back into her seat. "What are we toasting to, Maya?"

Without hesitancy, Maya raised her left hand and flashed a sparkling engagement ring.

"Goddamn!" China blurted. "What the hell is that?"

"That's one big ass ring, that's what that is," said Jade.

"I'm getting married," Maya announced, bubbling over with excitement.

"To whom? That one-night-stand in Orlando?" China took a swig of her champagne. "Girl, you done lost your damn mind." Leave it to China to pop Maya's bubble.

"I think it's wonderful!" Jade raised her glass to her sister. "Congratulations, Maya!"

Free remained quiet, but kept an eye on China who was releasing her green-eyed monster.

"Shit, I'm not toasting to a damn mistake," China barked.

"It's not a mistake," Maya shot back.

"No? Well, tell me, little sister, what in the fuck do you know about love when you've spent most of your adult life selling your ass?"

Jade and Free gasped and Veronica spat out her drink.

"Don't hate because no one will buy your dried up pussy!" Maya retorted. "You jealous bitch!"

"Okay," Free interjected. "Enough is enough. Your language is far too colorful for me."

"Pussy is in the dictionary, Free," said Jade.

"Maybe so, but I don't want to hear it. It's not lady like."

China tossed her head back and emptied her flute. She refilled it and turned to Maya. "Answer my question, girlie."

Maya rolled her eyes and mumbled under her breath.

"See?" China said, pointing at Maya. "She don't need to be marrying no damn body."

"Yes, I love him! There, are you fucking satisfied?"

"You're not in love. You're confusing him tapping that ass good with love."

"You're an evil wench, China." Maya sat her flute on the table. "You aren't happy unless someone else is miserable with your miserable old ass."

"Whatever, I'm happy for you. I just don't want you to make a mistake."

"Thank you, although I don't believe you."

Veronica wanted to relieve the tension, so she added her two cents. "Love is not an emotion, but a choice. We choose to love. The butterflies, the stir of excitement, and the emotions are not love, but lust and infatuation."

"That's bullshit," China said.

"It may be," Veronica said, "it may be not. People throw the L-word around like they throw around shit, fuck, and damn. Sometimes, all it takes is a good pipe laying that will make you want to scream out love you, knowing damn well you don't love his ass, but you love that dick!" Veronica fell out with laughter and refilled her glass.

"That's bullshit, and whoever told you that shit, tell them to kick rocks," said China.

"Love," Free started, "is giving without expecting anything in return."

"I agree, Free, which confirms my point that love is not an emotion but a choice," said Veronica.

"Love or not, I'm marrying Reggie. I am not going to let that rich motherfucker out of my grasp. That's it. That's all."

Jade shook her head and hissed at Maya. "That's awful. Listen, you can have all the money in the world and still be unhappy. So, it ain't the money, honey. Trust me."

"Yeah, okay, like it was actually Jon's dick that transformed your ass from pussy to dick," China said, chuckling.

"You all are so vulgar," Free hissed. Although annoyed with the language, she was actually enjoying the dialogue. For once, it was a healthy exchange, but only in the style of the Howard sisters.

Jade ignored China and said, "What happens when the butterflies, the stir of emotions and the lust are gone, but I still love him anyway?"

Veronica refilled her glass before responding. "You choose to stay with him, right?"

"Yeah, but I'm sure the millions of people that have had their hearts broken would have chosen not to fall in love with the asshole that broke their heart." Jade laughed hysterically while refilling her glass. "So, I feel it's an emotion. I loves me some Jon Meadows. Hell, I love that man's dirty drawers."

"You love his money," China said.

Jade sipped from her glass and shook her head. "Nope, not at all. Remember, I am Director of Human Resources. I am not hurting for money. In fact, Jon does not pay my bills. I pay my own shit."

"Love is an emotion," Maya said.

Veronica turned to Maya and said, "You see, I think it harbors both. We make the decision to love, which is often driven by emotion. Consequently, we opt out of love for the same reasons—neglect, betrayal, incompatibility, etc."

"Love don't control me, I control my damn self," barked China with a tongue thick as leather.

"It sounds like y'all are talking in circles to me," said Free. "True love comes from heaven and everything else isn't real."

"What? You're kidding me, right?" said Jade.

"No, I'm not. Now, don't get me wrong. I love my Sam, but I love God more."

"That's a different kind of love, Free," said Maya.

"Yes, it is. The love we get from God is the purest love. No man could ever give you that kind of love. The more I listen to Veronica, the more I'm inclined to agree with her. I choose to be with Sam; therefore, I choose to love him."

Maya blurted, "And y'all choose to fuck like rabbits, too," which ensued an uproar of laughter that Free didn't take too kindly.

After five bottles of alcohol, the women were wasted! However, Veronica didn't forget the real reason why she was aboard Jon*Air*.

"Now that we all are feeling breezy, I have something especially for you, Jade," Veronica announced, slowly standing, trying to steady her legs. Her head was woozy and knees wobbly. It was completely safe to assume that Veronica was fucked up. Nevertheless, she had a job to do and she was going to do it. In her many years of working for Meadows & Meadows, she never disappointed her boss.

"Uh, okay…what do you have?" asked Jade.

Veronica leaned in to Jade and pressed her index finger against her lips. "Shhh, it's a surprise." She stood up and waved her index finger. "Just wait, you'll see," she said in sing-song fashion.

Jade looked at her cross-eyed. "Did she just put her finger on my lips?"

Veronica moved toward the back of the plane.

China fell out with laughter. "Uh huh, and she shushed your ass, too. I like her."

"That bitch is crazy," said Maya.

"Hush," Jade said to Maya. "Don't call her a bitch. She's a nice person, she's just—"

"Fucked up, that's all," confirmed Free.

All eyes immediately shot to Free. They stared at her with the look of surprised plastered all over their faces.

"What? Y'all can say it, why can't I?"

They all fell over with laughter, almost hysterically.

Veronica returned with a humongous box wrapped in red velvet topped with the biggest red bow they'd ever seen.

"Wow!" Maya gasped, glaring at the box. "What's that?"

Veronica sat the box on the table in front of Jade. "Oh, you'll see in a few," Veronica said, taking her seat across from Jade.

With eyes wide as golf balls, Jade stared at the box. "What in the world…is this for me?"

Veronica nodded and reached for the remote control velcroed on the side of the table.

Jade reached for the box and Veronica snapped, "Wait!" Jade withdrew her hand like a scolded child. "Be patient. It'll be well worth it. Trust me, honey."

Veronica pointed the remote toward the flat screen television and turned it on. Jon's handsome face appeared. "Glad you could join us," said Veronica.

"It's my pleasure," he said.

Jade jumped at the sound of his voice. "Jon?"

"Hi, baby."

The sisters all swiveled around in their seats, and glared at the flat screen. The looks on their faces were priceless, which is exactly what Jon was aiming for.

"Jon, uh…what's going on, baby?" asked Jade, smiling from ear to ear.

In his office, Jon sat behind the massive oak desk, reclining in the leather high back executive chair. He loosened his tie. Jon possessed an air of calm and self-confidence, which Jade adored. Not much ruffled his feathers.

"My love, I miss you dearly," he said, looking into the webcam positioned on his laptop.

"I miss you, too, sweetie."

"Veronica, I take it everything's in place."

"Yes, Jon, it is."

"Hello, ladies," he spoke to the sisters, breaking their gaze and silence.

"Hi, Jon," they responded in unison.

He smiled and cleared his throat. He'd always surprised Jade with gifts, but this was sure to be a mega surprise that she will never, ever forget. "Jade, in front of you is a box."

She looked at the television and then at Veronica. She leaned over and whispered, "Can he see me?"

"Yes, I can see and hear you quite well, baby," he chuckled. "I can see that you all are having a grand time with the wet bar."

Jade's mouth dropped open. She tried to regain her composure and set upright in the seat. Of course, she was toasted. "Yes, we love the wet bar," she smiled, feeling awkward. The fact that Jon had microphones planted throughout the plane bothered her. Was he listening to their crazy conversation about love? Desperately, she tried to play the video loop in her mind but couldn't recall any of her comments or input in the conversation.

"Darling, I wrapped the box myself," he said.

"Did you? You did a beautiful job."

"Okay, now I know you're anxious to know what's in the box."

"Well, just a wee bit."

"We all are a wee bit anxious to see what's in this big ass box," said China.

Jon chuckled. "Well, I won't keep you waiting any longer. Baby, I love you more than words can express. You mean the world and more to me, Jade. I just can't imagine life without you—"

She heard his quick intake of breath. "I know you do, Jon. I love you so much too, baby."

"Girl, open the goddamn box!" China blurted out, now sitting on pins and needles.

Jade gazed from China to the flat screen.

"Open the box," Jon authorized.

Jade stared at the box, almost afraid to touch it. Now annoyed, China grabbed the bow and pulled it off the box.

"China!" Free snapped. "Mind your place."

"Mind my place? You need to get you some damn children."

Jade pulled off the top and saw another box. She looked at the flat screen. Jon nodded and smiled. Jade pulled off the top to see another box. She looked at the flat screen again. "Okay, what's going on?"

"Girl," Maya interjected. "I've seen this done before. Keep opening those boxes until you get to your gift!" Maya was more excited than Jade.

Finally, after pulling tops off of twenty boxes, Jade retrieved a tiny black velvet ring-sized box, with a gold bow wrapped around it. Her body stiffened. She looked at the flat screen.

Veronica, sitting back and smiling like the cat that swallowed the canary, was now sipping Ciroc and Cranberry.

"Sweetheart," Jon said, getting up from his desk, pushing his chair back, and getting down on one knee.

"Oh my God!" Maya said.

"My, my, my," said Free, shaking her head.

"My, my, my," mimicked China.

Surprisingly, Jade's hand was as steady as a surgeon's, holding the tiny box with care. Her auburn dreadlocks were twisted at the back of her head into a messy knot that suited the roundness of her face. As she looked at the flat screen, her eyes held narrow concentration.

"Baby, will you marry me?"

A pool of tears streamed down her bronzy cheeks. She nodded her head frantically, words lodged in her throat.

"Is that a yes," he asked, smiling widely.

"Yes!" Free, China and Maya responded for her in unison.

"Yes," she finally answered, wiping tears from her eyes.

"I wish I were there to put it on your finger," he said.

"Allow me," Maya said, taking the box from her sister. Jade looked at China, her eyes brightened with pleasure. "You so deserve this, sis."

Jade extended her left hand and Maya slid the 10-carat yellow white diamond. She was speechless.

"You like it?" asked Veronica.

"It's…it's so much…I don't need all of this," she said, looking toward Jon. "Thank you, baby."

"Yes, you need that and so much more. Baby, life for us has only just begun. I promise you, it will only get better. Well, I'll let you ladies get back to your fun. Enjoy LA and I'll talk to you later. I love you," he said, blowing her a kiss.

"I love you, too."

"Thanks, Veronica," he said.

"Anytime, boss!" With the remote, Veronica turned off the flat screen. She sat the remote on the table and picked up the bottle of Ciroc. "This calls for a drink and celebration. Oh yeah, and shopping on Rodeo Drive!"

"Here! Here!" were the responses, as champagne flutes tapped the bottle of Ciroc.

Maya held up her engagement ring. "Us's gettin' married now!"

CHAPTER 27

There is nothing worse than a drunken woman times three. The sight in the cabin was beholding—Maya was drooling, Jade was slumped over with her face pressed against the table, China was snoring, and Free looked at them with disgust. Although, she had to admit it was quite a funny sight. Besides, she was happy her sisters were able to be in the same room without killing each other for once.

The wheels gripped the tarmac as Jon*Air* landed, waking them from their drunken stupor. Quick on her feet, Veronica made a beeline for the front of the plane. She looked out the portal window and saw the awaiting limousine.

"We're here, ladies," she yelled. "Get up, now. We mustn't waste one minute of this beautiful day!"

Jade pulled herself upright and looked out the portal window. She focused her eyes and looked around the tarmac. She had never been to Los Angeles, but she had a strange feeling she wasn't in LAX. The surroundings looked too familiar.

"What the…Veronica! Veronica!"

Like the dutiful servant, Veronica rushed to Jade's side. "Yes'sum," she said in her best southern drawl voice followed by a stifled giggle. "Yes'sum, Missy Jade. I's here, Missy Jade. I's here."

Jade smirked. "That's real funny. We are not in Los Angeles, are we?"

"Nope, we're not in Kansas, Dorothy," she giggled.

"Where are we?"

"Montego Bay, Jamaica!"

Free stood up. "Jamaica!"

"Who said Jamaica? What about Jamaica?" Maya's tongue was as thick as pea soup.

China looked on dumfounded.

"Okay, Veronica, I am not getting off this plane until you tell me what's going on," Jade demanded.

"I can't tell you. So, why don't you just pull your little self off this plane because we have somewhere to be."

"I'm not going anywhere." Jade folded her arms across her chest and poked out her bottom lip.

"Well then, I suppose that's your choice." With a stern expression, Veronica turned on her heels and walked toward the plane. "Anyone else want to see Montego Bay?"

Maya was first to speak. "I'm right behind you."

China looked at Free and they both looked at Jade. "Well, as long as we're here," said China, getting out of her seat, snatching up her Louis Vuitton hobo bag, and heading toward the front of the plane.

China looked over her shoulder and smiled at Jade. "Just go with the flow, honey. It ain't like we've got a choice."

In a huff, Jade pulled herself up from her seat, swung her Dooney & Burke across her shoulder, and with a swimming head, followed behind everyone else. She smelled a rat and its name was Jon Meadows. Then, a smile graced her lips. *What does this man have up his sleeve now?* She loved Jon's surprises. She loved Montego Bay. But she'd never been to Los Angeles before and she was aching to break in the new credit card Jon had given her on Rodeo Drive.

As the women settled back into the black limousine, Jade reminisced on the first time she arrived in Montego Bay. A smile graced her face. "Man, talk about memories," she said, tuning her gaze toward Veronica.

Veronica knew exactly what she meant. "Girl, don't even remind me." She laughed, shaking her head. "We were torn up from the floor and them some!" Her chuckle turned into hysterical laughter. "Do you remember," she said, trying to catch her breath, "when Jon found us on the plane?"

With a warm smirk on her face, Jade nodded her head slowly. "I'll never forget it. Hell, he won't let me forget it."

"What happened?" asked Maya.

"Well, you see, what had happened was…" Veronica paused, followed by an eruption of laughter.

"I was kidnapped," Jade remembered.

Free looked at her strangely. "Kidnapped?"

Jade nodded her head. "Yup! Veronica whisked me away to Montego Bay on Jon's orders."

"Oh, I remember you telling me about that," said China.

"Yeah, but you don't even know the half of it, I'm sure," said Veronica.

"I'm all ears," said China, trying to listen intently with a serious buzz.

"On the flight, we ate three lobsters a piece, drank three bottles of Dom Perignon, and took several shots of Jose Cuervos."

"Damn!" cried Maya, wondering what happened to her lobster.

"To make a long story short, Jon and Paul had to carry Veronica and me off the plane."

"Paul?"

"Paul is Jon's brother," Veronica told Free, "and a gigantic asshole."

"Ahh, but that 'gigantic asshole' was the love of your life," added Jade.

"*Was* is the operative word here." Veronica rolled her eyes.

"Anyway," Jade continued, "I had gotten so drunk, I could barely walk. Jon had to carry me to the car.

"Yeah, and then she stuck her head out the window like a dog," Veronica teased, followed by another eruption of laughter.

"That's real classy," China said.

"Yeah, your sister added a new dimension to class when she threw up with her hanging outside the window!"

"Oh, that is disgusting," Free said, followed by laughter.

Jade laughed and exhaled deeply. "And it has never been boring since with Jon."

The limo pulled up in front of a nineteenth century, twenty-acre estate, surrounded by a private beach. So excited, Maya did not wait for the driver to open the door for her. She climbed out and stood with her mouth opened so wide, the salty air dried her throat.

She cleared her throat. "Beautiful. Absolutely beautiful."

"Yes, it surely is," Free said, standing behind her.

"This is truly a treat," China said, flanked at Maya's side.

As Jade and Veronica climbed out of the limo, the front door opened and out came Jon Meadows.

"Welcome to Meadowland, ladies!"

"Meadowland? Sounds like an amusement park," China chuckled.

Veronica pulled up beside China. "That's exactly what Jade said when she arrived for the first time."

Stunned to see her man, Jade blurted, "Jon Meadows! What are you doing here? I thought you were in New York. What's going on?"

Jon briskly walked toward his woman and took her into a familiar embrace, one she wished would never end. "Hello, my love. You know I can't be away from you for longer than a minute." He smiled widely, flashing his straight pearly whites. He kissed her on the neck, sending spirals of ecstasy through her.

She giggled. "Watch it, now. You know where this always leads."

"Get a room, you two," Veronica said, smiling.

"Hello, Ronnie," said Jon, "and thank you for everything." He leaned in and kissed her on the cheek. "You know you're the best, right?"

She smiled. "Yes, I know, and you're welcome."

Jon points toward white sand and turquoise blue water with snow-white waves brushing against the shore. "That's our private beach to use at your leisure, ladies."

"You mean private as in no one can see me if I choose to run naked?"

"Well, yes, unless there's a helicopter or plane hovering over, then they'll see your beauty," Jon told Maya with a smile.

Maya blushed and looked away. A part of her longed for Reggie, and imagined how wonderful it would've been to actually partake of sex on a beach. She sighed heavily and pushed the thought out of her mind. Reggie was in Florida.

Or so she thought. "Hey, baby girl!" the familiar voice yelled, walking out of the house and toward his woman.

"Reggie? Oh my, God! What are you doing here?" Maya dropped her bags and kicked rocks, running toward her man. She leapt into his arms and planted her lips against his, ravishing his mouth.

"What in the world?" said Free, looking at China. "What's going on? How did he and Jon get here?" China remained quiet. Free faced Jon. "Uh, how did you get here, Superman? I don't see your cape. Didn't we just chat with you on the plane, via webcam, not more than three hours ago?"

Jade looked at Jon, also seeking an answer.

Jon chuckled and lowered his head. "Okay, you caught me."

"Caught you doing what?" asked Jade.

Jon shoved his hands in his pant pockets. "Well, I wasn't actually in New York when Ronnie called from the plane."

Jade whipped around and faced Veronica.

Veronica pressed her lips tightly and looked up at the sky. "It sure is a beautiful day!"

"Honey," Jon continued, "come inside and I'll explain it all to you."

"No, you'll explain it now," she said, dropping her bag to the ground, making a statement that she wasn't moving unless he fessed up.

"Alright, I'll tell—"

"Hey, woman!" came from the front door.

Free spun around and saw Sam. Her mouth flew open, her words lodged in her throat.

"Hey, Mom!" Ashley and Andre said in unison, following behind Sam.

"Hey, babies," China said, her arms stretched wide open. They flew into her embraced and she kissed each on the forehead. "Did you enjoy the flight?"

"Yes!" they said.

Free whipped around and looked at China with surprise. "You knew about this, China?"

China smiled. "Guilty."

"Okay, let's go inside and get freshened up. The staff has prepared a wonderful beachside feast for us," said Jon.

"But, how did you all get here before us?" asked Jade.

"I'll explain everything over lunch." He kissed her on the cheek and ushered her inside the house.

CHAPTER 28

The ten-foot long table was covered with a blue table cloth reminiscent of the surf. Tall white pillar candles, with silver beads, on metal trays surrounded by seaside treasures like driftwood, pebbles, sea glass, shells and lilies were centerpieces for the beachside feast of steamed crab, Dungeness crab, Alaskan king crab, shrimp, clams, crab cakes, calamari, salmon, corn on the cob, coleslaw, roasted red potatoes, Caesar salad, and Jade's favorite, Dom Perignon.

Snow white waves crashed against the shore while Andre and Ashley waded in the clear blue water.

China sipped her water, looking over the rim of her glass at Jon. He nodded and smiled, holding tightly to Jade's hand who was conversing with Free.

China cleared her throat. Using her fork, she tapped her water glass. "May I have everyone's attention, please?" Laughter and conversation ceased; all eyes were on China. "I know my sisters are wondering what's going on." She stood up. "Well, this was all my idea."

"Your idea, China?"

"Yes, Free. It was all my idea." She looked at Jon. "And Jon's idea, too."

Jade looked at Jon with curiosity.

"Jon reached out to me," China continued, "in an attempt to understand the dynamics of the Howard sisters. Well, I don't quite understand it myself. All I know is that I love my sisters and I know my sisters love me, but we all have a crazy ass way of showing it."

"Here, here," chanted Free.

"So, after a long and wonderful conversation with Jon—who, by the way Jade, is a wonderful man and you are a very lucky woman—we came up with the idea of an intervention. We knew...no, *I* knew it would be tough rounding you all up for an intervention, especially coming from me, so Jon suggested we enlist the help of Veronica."

"Yes, when China called me and told me the plan, I was ready to do whatever she needed me to do. You see, I had sisters once—"

"Once?" said Jade.

Veronica inhaled and nodded her head. "My sisters, Vivian and Dorothy, were killed in a horrible car crash ten years ago and I've never felt lonelier in my life, and still do. Of course, you all aren't going to agree on everything, but...well, I wish I had my sisters with me." She lowered her head and wept silently.

Sitting next to Veronica, Maya wrapped her arm around her, consoling her. "Well, sister, you have four sisters right here. You're alright with me, Veronica."

"Thank you, Maya." Veronica smiled.

"I must admit, though, I was a little hesitant," said Jon. "By my not being a part of the family, I didn't feel right getting involved—"

"Nonsense!" blurted Free. "The way you love on my sister, you will always be a part of this family. Jade is happier than she'd ever been in a long time, and that is all because of you."

"Yeah, and all that money," Maya chimed in.

"I don't see your man working at Dairy Queen, Maya," Free retorted.

Reggie raised his glass of Dom Perignon. "Here, here," he said, followed by a chuckle. "I couldn't take care of my baby on a Dairy Queen salary."

Maya twisted her neck and playfully rolled her eyes. "You've got that right!"

Laughter ensued, and China tapped her glass once again. "I'd like for us all to play a game."

"And that's my cue," Veronica said, standing. "I have a plane to catch."

"Where are you going?" asked Jade.

"But we haven't started yet," said China.

"Yes, and I thought we were going to Los Angeles to pick out a house, and—"

"Work is calling and I have no time for games. Besides I have to get back to New York," she faced Jade, "you're right where you need to be at the moment. We'll touch bases when you return to New York. Have a wonderful time, everyone!"

"Alright then…" Jade trailed off, disappointment heavy in her voice.

"Come give me a hug," said China. "It was so good meeting you. I look forward to hanging out with you again."

With a smile, Veronica accepted China's embrace, as well as the warm, appreciative hugs from Free and Maya.

Jade remained in her seat, still disappointed because Veronica had become a dear close friend, but she waved her off and blew hew a sisterly kiss. "Be safe, sweetie. I will call you when I get back."

"Will do," she said and she was off.

They all watched as Veronica disappeared into the house.

"What kind of game?" asked Free, breaking the silence.

"Games are for children," said Maya.

"See? That's it right there," said China. "Why can't you just have an open mind?"

Maya was about to speak until Reggie shot her a hush-your-mouth look. China caught it and said, "Thank you, Reggie."

Maya stuck out her tongue at China.

"Anyway, the game is called Getting to Know You. Now, the game is easy. I think it will be fun and interesting. Tell the person to your right how you feel about them."

"That sounds easy enough," said Jade.

"It really is. So, I'll start." Maya sat to her right. *Oh goodness. God, this was your plan. You made sure she sat on my right, didn't*

You? Oh well, here goes. "Maya, I envy you." Maya's eyes widened. China chuckled. "Yeah, I know, right? But, you know what, in all seriousness, I really do admire your independence. I wish I had the wherewithal you have. When you left home and hitchhiked three thousand miles to California to pursue your dreams, inside I was very proud of you and also very afraid for your safety."

Opened mouths surrounded the table, as her sisters could not believe their ears. Maybe this game was a great idea after all. Clear the air, cleanse the soul.

"About two weeks ago before your last visit to Orlando," China continued, "and I know it was wrong for me to do so, but I paid Reggie a little visit."

Maya's eyes widened. "You did what?"

"Calm down, honey." Reggie put his hand on her shoulder.

"But how?" Maya asked, looking perplexed.

"You left his address programmed in my GPS."

"You sneaky–"

"Okay, don't go there, Maya!" Free interrupted. "And that goes double for you, too, China."

Everyone broke into laughter.

Maya couldn't help from giggling, too. "So, why did you do it?"

"Because like I said…" China paused, clearing her throat, "I was concerned about your safety and I wasn't about to see you make another mistake."

Everyone sat in disbelief while China and Reggie explained the conversation they had that day about her concern for Maya's well-being. Reggie assured China that he had every intention to do right by Maya. Although he was aware of Maya's checkered past and she aware of his, he loved her deeply and more than any woman he had ever met.

Maya, usually outspoken, was speechless and near the brink of tears. "You two have known each other all this time?"

"Yes," China said, smiling while Reggie held Maya's hand. "And since Jon and I were planning this family get together, I had to include him on the details."

"Oh my God," Maya said, unable to hold back her tears anymore.

"I love you, Maya. And as much as I give you grief, nobody else better give you any grief." She looked at Reggie. "Reggie, I still don't know you from a can of paint, but you've made my sister quite happy. So, if she likes it, I love it. But do know that if you so much as lift a finger against her and hurt her in any way," she looked around the table, "your ass will wind up missing."

Once again, Reggie raised his glass. "Understood," he said with a smile. He looked at Maya and kissed her on the cheek.

China raised her glass, took a sip, sat down, reached for a crab ball, and popped it in her mouth.

"I guess it's my turn," said Maya. She took a deep breath and smiled the biggest smile anyone had ever seen. She faced Reggie and took his hand in hers. "Baby, where do I start? I've never been more in love with anyone as I am with you. In a short time, you taught me what true love really is and how to value it. You are strong, loving, caring, and the best lover I've ever had. You, Reginald Anthony Hamilton, complete me."

Free's lips parted in surprise. She'd never, ever heard Maya speak so lovingly toward anyone. "That was beautiful, Maya," she said, smiling at her baby sister. Was Maya finally maturing? Yes she was and right before her eyes. Sometimes all it takes is the right person to bring out the best in someone.

It was now Reggie's turn. He turned to his right and looked at Free. "It has been a pleasure meeting you, Ms. Free. I promise you that I will take very good care of your sister." He then looked at China. "I don't want to come up missing." Everyone chuckled. "She will never want for anything and, as long as I have anything to do with it, her heart with never ache."

"For your life, you better hope so," said China with a stern look. "That's our baby you've got in your grasp, and if—"

Reggie raised his hand in surrender. "Trust me. I love this woman right here. You have nothing to worry about."

"Well, with that said," Free turned to Sam, "I love you more than life itself, and I never thought I could love anyone or anything like this other than my sisters. You have changed my life. You have changed me. You have made me a better woman, and for that I thank you, Samuel. I love you so very much."

Sam's eyes studied Free with intensity. His heart was about to explode with all the love he had for her. He cupped her face and pulled her lips to his and softly kissed her. "I love you, too," he whispered. Gathering himself, he faced Jade. "Jade, you and I haven't spent much time together to really get to know each other, but I mimic Reggie's sentiments when I tell you that I love your sister and I promise you, China, and Maya that I will never stop loving her, and she will always be the center of my life."

"Thank you, Sam. It really means the world to me that Free has you to love her."

"Yeah, yeah, face your man, girlie," said Maya to Jade.

Jade rolled her eyes at Maya and faced Jon. She paused before she spoke, ensuring she chose the right words. "Being loved by you is powerful. Loving you will be forever. I can't wait to be your wife."

The "ahs" and "ohs" drowned out the waves crashing against the shore.

Jon flashed a broad smile. "Damn, woman," was all he could say, as he found himself without words. He gathered his composure and faced China.

"Well, Jon, I guess you have to tell China how you feel about her," Maya chuckled.

"Why do you find that funny, Maya?" asked China.

Maya shrugged her shoulders, not wanting to get into a let's-see-who-can-squirt-the-farthest match with China. She was too wrapped up into her man and not this damn game.

"Alright, sisters, we're having a wonderful time loving on each other, so let's keep it that way," said Jade. She stretched her arms above her head and released a sharp shrill. "I feel like getting in the water," she said, looking at Jon. "Naked," she squealed.

"Oh, I don't want to see that," said Maya.

China brought her champagne flute to her lips and echoed Maya's sentiments. "Same here."

"Well, I'm stuffed," said Free.

"Yes," said Sam, "this was some kind of feast, Jon. I can't thank you enough for everything."

"You're welcome, my brother. Anytime."

"I think I am going to gather up my kiddies and just relax. Maybe take a walk on the beach, clear my mind…"

"That sounds like a great idea," said Free. "Isn't it beautiful here?"

"Yes," said China, nodding her head. "I could so live here."

"Me too," said Maya. "I could be like LisaRaye."

"The First Lady you're not, and this ain't Turks or whatever it is," chuckled China, getting a dib at Maya. One good dib deserved another.

As Maya was fixing her mouth for a snappy, but probably crude comeback, Jade noted Paul, Jon's brother, coming out of the house and walking toward the group of catty women and their men.

"Hey, Paul!"

"Jade, how are you, sweetie?"

Jade stood and embraced Paul. "I'm doing wonderful. So glad to see you. Let me introduce you to my family."

"Hey, brother, good to see you," said Jon, embracing his sibling.

"Paul, this is my sister Free," she said, pointing across the table," and her fiancé Sam. That's my sister Maya and her fiancé Reggie and this is my sister China."

Paul smiled at China, his eyes held a sheen of purpose. He liked what he saw. *It's going to be a wonderful weekend after all*, he thought as he nodded his head toward her and said, "Nice to meet you China. No fiancé for you?"

Jade chuckled at his humor. "No, China is—"

"Single," China said matter-of-factly, interrupting Jade. A devilish look came into her eyes as she, too, liked what she saw.

Oh, Jesus, Jade thought, throwing Jon a look. *Here we go.*

"You just missed Veronica," said Jade to Paul.

With his eyes still plastered on China, he said, "That's too bad." His voice was low and smooth.

Jade followed his gaze to China and then back to him. "My dear, she'll be here all weekend," she chuckled, breaking his fixated trance. "Are you hungry? There's plenty of food."

"No, I'm good, thanks."

"Didn't know you were coming, brother," said Jon.

"It was last minute, but," he faced China, "I'm so glad I came."

Maya stood. "I hate to break up the party, but I think I want to take a swim. Babe, let's get changed."

On cue, Reggie stood and took his woman by the waist. "Sounds like a great idea, honey. Anyone care to join us?"

"You all enjoy yourselves," said Free. She looked at Sam. "I would like to take a walk and digest this food." Sam stood and pulled back her chair. "We'll see everyone later."

"On second thought, a swim sounds good," said Jade.

"Sounds good to me, too," said Jon.

"Great," said Maya. "We'll see you back here in about thirty minutes."

Paul took a seat at the table, across from China, his eyes peering through her soul.

Jon stood up and extended his hand toward Jade. "Come on, babe," he said.

Jade looked up at her man and smiled, placing her hand in his. "You're such a gentleman," she teased. Standing, she shot Paul and China and disgusting look.

As Jon and Jade were heading into the house, Jon's cell phone rung. The number was unfamiliar, but he took the call anyway.

"Jonathan Meadows," he answered. "Yes…What?" He stopped in his tracks. Jade stopped, too. "Are you sure?" His face hardened, reflecting pain. "Oh my God!"

"What's wrong?" she whispered, concerned by his slouching posture and look of pain and concern on his face. "What is it, Jon?"

"Thank you," he said, closing his cell phone. He shoved it in his pocket. He held back his head and dropped to his knees, crying hysterically.

"Oh my, God, Paul!" Jade cried out. "Come quick!" She got down on her knees and grabbed Jon around his shoulders. "Baby, what is it? What's wrong?"

He couldn't speak, choked by his tears.

Paul ran up to them, kicking sand, falling down to his brother's side. "What it is?"

"Oh my God," Jon cried, shaking his head. "I don't believe it!"

"You don't believe what, Jon. Please, you're scaring the shit out of me. What in the hell is going on?"

Jon held up his head and attempted to gather his composure. "Jon…" he paused, unable to get out the words. "Jon*Air*…"

"What about it?" Paul asked.

At the sound of Jon*Air*, immediately Jade's stomach muscle tightened into a ball. She slouched over for fear of Jon's forthcoming words.

"JonAir," he said, taking a deep breath and looking into his brother's eyes, "went down. Ronnie was on the plane."

Paul's body stiffened, feeling the screams of devastation at the back of his throat. His body jolted as if his life had been stolen. Although he and Veronica were no longer together, she remained the love of his life, and losing her was devastating blow to his heart.

CHAPTER 29

A cloud of sadness hovered over the heavily ethnic-decorated living room with a white baby grand positioned in the corner.

Jade sat on the edge of the sofa, embraced by Jon. "What happened, Jon?" she cried. "Why did the plane crash? I don't understand?"

"I don't know," he said repeatedly, mourning the woman who had been by his side since the beginning of Meadows & Meadows Architecture. She was his blackberry, ensuring he was where he needed to be at all times. She was his therapist. She truly was a best friend, and now she was gone. His heart ached more than ever before.

"That could've been us," said Maya, looking off into the distance. "We could've been dead," she said, looking around the room at her sisters.

Jade peered at Maya, her mouth taking on an unpleasant twist. "That is so insensitive of you, Maya!" she snapped, her eyes now seething with anger. "All you can think of is your selfish behind!"

Maya was taken aback. "No," she started, but was stopped by the squeeze of Reggie's hand on her thigh. She looked at him. "But that's now that I meant."

He leaned in and whispered into her ear. "I know, babe. I know."

"I'm sure that's not what she meant," Free said, speaking up in defense of her sister.

"I was just saying that—"

"Keep your thoughts to yourself, Maya!" Jade cried, jerking to her feet. "You just make me sick!" she spewed, rushing out of the living room, past China who stood frozen in the doorway.

"Jade?" she called out after her. She walked up to Free. "What happened now?"

Free took a deep sigh and looked at Maya.

Maya felt their stairs burning through her. "I didn't do anything!" she cried, and rushed out of the living room as well.

"I'll make sure she's okay," Reggie said, following behind her.

Jon stood, trying to gather his composure. "Guess I better go check on Jade. She and Ronnie were very close," he said, his voice cracking.

Paul sat in the corner of the sofa, tightly hugging a pillow, holding a blank stare. China's heart ached for him as she knew his pain all too well.

"Well, I'm a little exhausted," Free said, looking at Sam. "I'd like to take a nap. You coming?" Sam nodded and caressed her arm. "China, I'll see you later?"

"Yes," China whispered, her gaze fixated on Paul.

Once Free and Sam had disappeared to their room, China eased up beside Paul and took a seat.

"I understand," she said. "I understand how you feel."

With a tear-stained face, Paul sat silent.

She settled back into the sofa and grabbed a pillow and pulled it into her chest. "Yes," she continued, "I know all too well the pain you're feeling." She shook her head, trying her best not to travel down memory lane.

Still staring forward, he mumbled, "You don't know how I feel."

She released a slight chuckle. "If that were only true. You see, I buried my husband a few weeks ago." Paul faced her, his eyes now held compassion for her. She pressed her lips tightly, trying to suppress the cry wanting to escape. "The only difference here is that my husband committed suicide."

"I'm so sorry to hear of this," said Paul, now turning his torso toward her.

"Thank you."

"Was he ill?"

"Who, my husband?"

"Yes," he whispered.

As much as she tried to suppress it, that damn tear made its way out and down her cheek. One simply cannot suppress something that's meant to be.

Paul noticed the tear and wiped it way. His act of kindness and compassion startled her.

"My husband..." she paused. "Well, he liked men."

Paul's back straightened.

"But you know what, Paul? I no longer feel like any of it was my fault. I was a good wife. I am a good woman. I gave him all he needed and so much more. I wouldn't say that Ron, that's my husband, had a sickness, but rather he lived a lie for twenty years."

"Wow," was all he could muster. He felt sorry for her, wanted to reach out and kiss away her hurt and pain. He caressed her face. "You deserve better than that," he said, leaning in closer.

This was wrong and she knew it, but she was craving it. She needed to feel the touch of a man. She needed to feel that she was still desired by a man. "Paul, I—"

He kissed her opened mouth with passion, and without hesitation, she surrendered. It felt good to them both and much needed. They understood each other's pain and only they could remedy their hurt, if only for an hour.

Paul leaned gently stroked her bottom lip with his tongue. Cupping her face, he covered her mouth, taking hold of her tongue, sucking tenderly. China inched closer to him and held on tight. He kissed her face, her ear, the back of her neck.

"Oooooh," she cooed as he lingered there, damn near driving her out of her mind.

Her body shuttered from the chills raging throughout her.

His hands roamed all over her body, finally nesting between the warm of her uncovered thighs. His fingers inched under her shorts. He found what he sought as he fingered the toy in her sandbox, bringing her to a full climax.

She stifled her cries of ecstasy as best she could, but her cries were heard by Jade as she stood frozen in the foyer. She watched as Paul crawled to the floor, bringing China down with him. She shook her head as she watched her future brother-in-law pull off her sister's shorts and toss them across the room. She was appalled as China's legs automatically wrapped around his neck as he partook of her goodies. Something in her wanted to scream with disgust when she heard China say, "Eat that pussy, baby!"

Quietly, Jade backed up toward the steps and flew up them like a bat out of hell toward the room she shared with Jon. Once inside, she closed the door behind her; plastering her back against it with her hand gripping the doorknob.

Jon looked up from his book and her eyes were hard, cold, and distant. "Babe, you okay?" He tossed the book on the bed and rushed toward her. "Girl, you look like you've just seen a ghost."

She looked into his eyes and shook her head. "China and Paul are fucking on the living room floor," she whispered.

"What? Are you sure?"

"Yes! I know what I saw! How could she do that?"

Jon pulled her into an embrace. "Jade, calm down." He tried to make sense of it all. He led her to the edge of the bed and sat down with her. "You know, baby, they both have been through something traumatic. China just buried her husband and Paul just lost Ronnie."

"It just happened today, not more than a few hours ago, Jon. You're accepting of this?"

"No, of course not, sweetie. But Paul and China are two adults. Who are we to judge them or control their lives? I'm just saying—"

Jade raised her up her hand. "Veronica was my friend."

"She was my friend, too. Are China and Paul right in what they're doing? Maybe not, but people have to find a way to ease the pain they best way they know how."

"Yes, I guess you're right, but it just doesn't seem right to me."

"Listen, we have full day tomorrow and I have surprise for everyone. So, let's get to bed!"

"Oh goodness, Jon, I don't think I can take any more of your surprises." She chuckled, took off her robe and climbed into bed.

Jon pulled up behind her and kissed her neck. "You know I love you, right?"

She patted his arm. "Of course, I do, silly."

Jade kissed her man's hand and closed her eyes, trying to push China and Jon from her mind.

"Hey, babe?"

"Hmm."

"Suppose China and Paul were to get married?" he chuckled.

"Oh shut up, Jon, and go to sleep!"

CHAPTER 30

The following morning, the group met in the front of the estate. Paul and China acted as though they didn't know each other from a can of paint. But Jade knew better as she eyed them behind her dark shades. The lime green straw hat shaded the smirk on her face from others. All except Free, making it her business to be overly protective and just downright nosey when it came to her sisters.

She pulled up beside Jade. "I want that dress," she said, eyeing the sheer multi-colored sheath covering a hot pink slip dress.

"What? This old thing?"

Free chuckled. "What is up Jon's sleeve today?" she asked, looking at everyone anxiously standing around and waiting on Jon to exit the house.

"I don't know, girl, but whatever it is, be prepared for a doozy. Jon Meadows does nothing half-assed, that's for sure." Jade sighed heavily and switched her weight from her left to her right, sticking out her right foot and tapping it.

Acknowledging Jade's demeanor, Free asked one simple question that would open up a box of regurgitation from the night before. "What's wrong, Jade?"

Jade grabbed her by the hand and pulled away from the group. She crossed her arms over her chest and shook her head.

"What?" Free asked again.

"Girl, why did I come downstairs last night to see China and Paul doing the nasty?"

Free recoiled and gasped. "You're kidding me."

Jade shook her head. "Nope, and I just feeling like vomiting every time I think about it."

Free was speechless. She couldn't find the words to speak the jumbled thoughts running rampant through her mind. All she could do was shake her head with her mouth opened wide, drying out her throat.

She cleared her throat. "But why would she do something like that? That is so not like her. That's more like Maya."

Jade frantically nodded her head as if she'd just answered the million dollar question. "Exactly! From Paul, it doesn't surprise me. He's such a whore, but from China?"

"What did she say when you saw her?"

"She didn't know I was there. She was too busy telling him to eat that pussy."

Free gasped. "My word!"

"What about Jon, does he know?"

Jade nodded her head.

Free stared at her, waiting for a verbal response. When she didn't receive one, she barked, "Well?"

"He said, 'they were two grown folks and we should just mind our business. We shouldn't judge them,' or some shit like that."

Free looked over at China. "Uh huh, no wonder she's been so quiet this morning." She then looked over at Paul. "Look, he don't even know what to do with his self."

"I know, right?"

Just then, Maya looked over at Free and Jade huddled next to huge purplish-blue flowers in the shape of snowballs. Jade clashed with her lime green and hot pink.

Jade spotted Maya peering at them. "Ut oh, I see trouble."

Free followed Jade's stare. "Ut oh is right."

The both laughed in Maya's direction, which gave her permission to move toward them.

"Shit," said Free. "Here she comes."

"I heard that, Free. Yeah, here I come," Maya chuckled. "What y'all doing over here away from everyone else?" Maya was loud and boisterous, which snagged China's attention.

"Damn, you're loud!" snapped Jade.

Her curiosity was piqued and she wanted in on the fun, too. China rushed over to the group and smiled. "What's going on, y'all?"

"Nasty! Just plain ol' nasty," said Free. She couldn't help herself. Being the Mother Hen that she was, she had to confront China.

"What are you talking about?" asked Maya.

"Good question," said China, looking at Free as if she'd just succumbed to Alzheimer's.

"What you did last night was despicable, China. You should be ashamed of yourself!" she scolded, her eyes peering deep into China, not liking what her soul has become.

China's posture straightened. "I wish I could say that I knew what your crazy ass was talking about, but I can't and—"

"Paul," Jade interjected. "She's talking about your little sexcapade with Paul last night."

"Ooooooooweeeeeeeeeeee!" said Maya, plastering her hand over her mouth. Her eyes grew as big as golf balls.

China succumbed to the tongue lashing. Yes, she it was wrong, but they all had men in their lives. She had no one and it was what she needed. Why is that so bad as long as she's not hurting anyone?

"I'm grown and I do what I want to do," China snapped.

"Is that it? That's all you have to say?"

"Yes, Free, that's it, that's all, and mind ya goddamn business. I fuck who I wanna fuck, and you fuck who you wanna fuck, and we'll all be just fuckin' happy!" she screamed, followed by a well of emotions erupting into a pool of tears streaming down her face, leaving trails in her MAC foundation.

China's outburst caught the attention of the men. Surprisingly, Paul rushed to her side.

"Is everything all right, here?" Paul asked China, looking around at her sisters.

Just flabbergasted, a slew of insults formed in the pit of Jade's stomach, heading for her mouth, but stopping short of her throat when Jon exited from the house.

"Everyone ready to go?" he asked, moving toward the crowd that had now centered on China and Paul. Something didn't feel right. He looked at Jade.

As Jon moved closer toward the circle, Jade's demeanor softened and a forced smile replaced the look of hatred and despise for Paul.

"Good morning, folks!" Jon greeted the group, his eyes plastered on Jade. "Everything okay, baby?"

"Yes. Yes, everything's fine. Are you ready to go?"

"Yes, the car is—"

"No," China interjected, "everything is not fine. My sister seems to give a shit about whom I'm fucking, and I can't for the life of me understand why?"

"Ut ohs" and "whats" pierced through the crowd. Jon was dumbfounded and the look on his face spoke volumes.

Free propped her hands on her full hips. "Uh, China, that was not necessary and you know it."

"Well, let's just get the shit out in the open so the rest of our day will not be spoiled with whispering, nasty looks and shit talking behind my back." She faced Paul and smiled at him. "I had the best sex of my life last night and I, for one, do not regret it. Thank you, Paul, for making me feel desirable, sexy, and wanted. I hadn't felt that way in years."

Paul smiled and looked down at the plush grass beneath his feet. All were silent, waiting for his response. He shoved his hands in his pockets and sighed heavily. He then looked at every face in the crowd before landing his hazel eyes on China.

"You're welcome, China." He extended his hand to her. She placed her hand in his. "I would love to do it again." He tossed a flirtatious smile her way.

She received that smile and threw one back in return. "I'm always ready."

Jade huffed, turned on her heels, and walked away.

China fell out with laughter and looped her arm around Paul's arm. She looked at Jon. "Aww, don't worry about Debbie Downer. She'll get over it. Now, shall we get going? I'm so hungry, I could eat a dick!"

Free's mouth fell open and Maya fell out in a full hearty laughter.

CHAPTER 31

The driveway seemed to last forever before they pulled up in front of the luxury estate.

"Wow, this is beautiful," said China as they all piled out of the van.

Jade took off her shades and removed her hat. She looked up at the massive structure and took in its beauty. "It certainly is. Just amazing… Is this where we're having breakfast, honey, because I'm starved?"

Jon smiled at Jade and left her side, taking center stage in front of everyone.

"If I could have everyone's attention, please." He paused, waiting for everyone's undivided attention. He wanted to make sure they heard every single word he had to say. He took a deep breath and released a heavy sigh. "After what happened yesterday, this has now become a bittersweet moment for me." He looked to his right and pointed at the empty spot next to him. "Veronica should be standing right here as I make this speech, because this was all her idea. But…" he paused, appearing deep in thought, searching for his next word. "I know she's here in spirit."

The crowd mumbled words of "Yes she is" and "Amen."

Jon stretched his arms out wide. "Welcome to Crossing Sisters. It has two double slip wet boathouses and this is the main home. The five-bedroom, four-bath stone residence has oversize rooms, including a formal dining room, sun room, and two offices. With many lovely features, including white oak floors, natural wood finishes, and stone wood burning fireplace, the home has character surrounded by twenty acres of land, beaches, and recreational areas, including golf and skiing. The perfect getaway."

Reggie chuckled. "Man, you sound like my realtor. You trying to sell us this house or something?"

Everyone broke into laughter, including Jon.

"No, not trying to sell the house. In fact, I've already purchased it."

"You what?" Jade exclaimed.

"Yes. Do you like it?"

"Yes," Jade said. "It's beautiful. But you already have a house here. Why buy another one?"

Jon reached out for Jade. "Come here, babe." She tilted her head with curiosity and approached him, placing her hand in his. Jon extended his other hand. "I need your sisters by my side, too, please."

The threesome looked at each other and then at Jon. China was a bit hesitant, Maya was willing to throw caution to the wind as usual, and Free felt a little excitement in her tummy. They took their place beside Jon and looked at Jade. She shrugged her shoulders.

"Honey, what's this all about?" Jade asked Jon. She loved his surprises, but damn this was getting ridiculous!

"I purchased it, but the four of you own it."

"What?" asked Free.

"Get the fuck outta here," said Maya, grinning from ear to ear.

"Wait a minute," said Jade. "Jon, what do you mean we own it?"

Jon ran his fingers through his short, curly tresses. He looked up at the beautiful, cloudless blue sky, making sure to choose his words carefully. There was one thing he had learned about the Howard sisters. They will jump down your throat and then some if you so much as think about saying the wrong thing to them. Since dating Jade, he'd learned to tread lightly around her sisters, which is something Sam and Reggie must learn to do.

"Listen, the four of you are grown ass women and you need to grow the hell up and learn to play nicely with each other," is what he wanted to say, but that wouldn't be treading lightly. So, instead he said, "This is my wedding gift to you, babe. A place where you and your sisters can come to relax, meditate, or to simply be sisters. That's why I named it Crossing Sisters. It's time, sweet baby, for you and your sisters to cross over into adulthood—"

China cleared her throat. "I beg your pardon, Jon!"

"No," Sam said, stepping up to Free's side. "Jon's right. Y'all fuss, fight, and cuss each other out way too much for my taste."

"That's not true," Jade said while in the back of her mind she knew better.

"Yep, there's truth in it," said Reggie.

Maya snapped her head in Reggie's direction. "Say what? You ain't been in the family but a hot minute—"

Reggie pressed his index finger against her soft lips. "Hush, woman. That's your problem right there, you can't keep your mouth closed."

Maya gasped. "Reginald Anthony Hamilton! How dare you?"

He smiled and kissed his woman on the cheek. "What? How dare I tell you the truth? Babe, since we've been together, our phone conversations are always about some beef you're having with your sisters. It has to stop and it has to stop here and now. The four of you…you are all each other has. I wish I had a brother or sister."

Jon was absolutely right, and they all knew it, but only one of them didn't want to hear the truth. But, nonetheless, China kept her mouth closed.

Free nodded her head. "You're absolutely right!"

"So, this is our house. I mean estate?" Maya asked.

"Yes. Each one of your names is on the deed. It's paid in full. No mortgage."

"But the utilities are going to kill us," said Free.

Reggie wrapped his arm around his woman. "Naw, I'll take care of the household expenses as long as you ladies act like ladies, not children," he playfully scolded.

"Oh, baby!" Maya jumped up with glee and wrapped her arms around Reggie's neck, planting a passionate kiss on his lips and sneaking in a little tongue.

"Oh, get a damn room!" China blurted, followed by laugher. "Well, I, for one, love my new house and I'm hungry. Where's the kitchen. I'll fix us something to eat." She faced Jon. "Uh, bruh-in-law, there is food in the fridge, right?"

"Yep," said Paul, pulling up next to China. "I took care of that yesterday. And," he looked at Jade, "the basement is fully stocked with your favorite libation."

Free shook her head. "I hope you have Alcoholics Anonymous on this here plantation, because your girl's about to turn into a damn lush!"

They all fell out with laughter and walked arm-in-arm inside Crossing Sisters.

THE END...

Nah, these sisters are coming back!

ABOUT THE AUTHOR

JESSICA TILLES is the best-selling author of *Anything Goes, In My Sisters' Corner, Apple Tree, Sweet Revenge, Fatal Desire, Unfinished Business, Erogenous Zone: A Sexual Voyage, Loving Simone*, contributing author to *The Triumph of My Soul* with her short story "Julian's Grace," and *No One Has to Know*, an eQuickie.

Listed in Heather Covington's *Top 100 Literary Divas*, Jessica is the award-winning publisher of Xpress Yourself Publishing and Creative Director/Owner of TWA Solutions, a small, minority- and woman-owned business providing services to independent publishers and authors and small businesses in the areas of book design, editing, web design, consulting and self-publishing services.

Jessica is currently working on her next novel, and resides in Upper Marlboro, Maryland with her two dogs: Abby and Teddy.

Learn more about Jessica at the following sites:

www.JessicaTilles.com
www.XpressYourselfPublishing.com
www.TWASolutions.com

Xpress Yourself Publishing
A Publisher of Fine Books
and
2008 AALAS Independent Publishing House of the Year

Visit us online:
www.xpressyourselfpublishing.org

www.ingramcontent.com/pod-product-compliance
Lightning Source LLC
Chambersburg PA
CBHW031402250626
47155CB00004B/1380